T0067999

Jesus Cookies

Jesus Cookies

SARAH KELLY ALBRITTON

"And He said unto them; Go ye into all the world
and preach the Gospel to every creature."

Mark 16:15

WESTBOW
PRESS®
A DIVISION OF THOMAS NELSON
& ZONDERVAN

WestBow Press books may be ordered through booksellers or by contacting:

WestBow Press
A Division of Thomas Nelson & Zondervan
1663 Liberty Drive
Bloomington, IN 47403
www.westbowpress.com
1 (866) 928-1240

Because of the dynamic nature of the Internet, any web addresses or
links contained in this book may have changed since publication and
may no longer be valid. The views expressed in this work are solely those
of the author and do not necessarily reflect the views of the publisher,
and the publisher hereby disclaims any responsibility for them.

Any people depicted in stock imagery provided by Getty Images are
models, and such images are being used for illustrative purposes only.
Certain stock imagery © Getty Images.

Scripture quotations are from the ESV® Bible (The Holy Bible, English
Standard Version®), copyright © 2001 by Crossway, a publishing ministry
of Good News Publishers. Used by permission. All rights reserved.

ISBN: 978-1-9736-2249-9 (sc)
ISBN: 978-1-9736-2248-2 (e)

Print information available on the last page.

WestBow Press rev. date: 3/13/2018

This is the author's third book but unlike the first two, *The Other Side of the* **Flood** and *Embrace the Thorns*, is purely fictional except for a few stories about her own children and the names of a few friends and relatives given to some of the characters.

All of her children were raised with the purpose of glorifying God in mind, hence the title, Jesus Cookies. The message is to tell the story.

During the writing of this book, her third daughter Kristi Kuyrkendall, battled, and was healed of, colon cancer. Praise God from whom all blessings flow!

DEDICATION

I dedicate this book to the Clinton Christian
Academy girls' softball team and coaches, who
made my "Jesus Cookies" a household name.

Special thanks to my eldest daughter Kelli Irby, for her
hard work and technical support. Without her help and
encouragement there would absolutely be no book.

CHAPTER 1

*M*ary Elizabeth Buie dressed for church as she always did on Sunday morning. In pensive thought, she recalled the bright sun-shiny days gone by when her mood had not been so melancholy. Today she did not look forward to her usual short walk to the old Presbyterian Church on the corner of Main and Prospect streets. The war had just ended. It had been a gory struggle pitting brother against brother in a fight to the death. It was disturbing to see the pain and destruction to which each was willing to go to achieve their cause.

Reaching into her closet, Mary Elizabeth selected a baby blue and white dress with the tiniest buttons down the front. Not being quite old enough to have her dress cinched up at the waist like a saddle on a horse, she slipped into the dress and maneuvered the buttons herself. Her silk petticoat over crinoline made a hoop unnecessary as she had not yet mastered the art of sitting without her hoop flying up in the front. Beside her bed sat a petite pair of white shoes sporting white laces and bows. Slipping them on her feet, she tied the laces and began to look for her matching lace gloves. Her attire was standard for gentile southern ladies of the time. All the ado involved in the process did not seem to be a bother to them. "Now, my new bonnet." It was white with delicate little blue flowers around the crown and a matching blue bow that tied beneath her chin. Her long black curls fell forward from beneath her bonnet and cascaded over her shoulders. She pinched her cheeks slightly as she looked in the mirror, giving them a very lovely rose color.

Picking up her miniature silk purse, with the draw string at the top, she made her way to the front door.

"Mama, I will see you and Papa in front of the church. I want to meet Charlotte there."

"Be careful of your clothes." her mother responded.

Outside, the air hung heavy with the smell of smoke mingled with the stench of rotting flesh of horses that had been buried in very shallow graves.

"Blamed Yankees", she uttered almost to herself.

She scanned the street that only a short time before had been filled with happy people enjoying walks and the smell of sweet magnolia blossoms and honeysuckles. Elizabeth clinched her teeth and thought, "This doesn't even look like my home. My beautiful city burned like so much trash. Why? Our armies had been defeated."

As she continued her walk and her lament, she noticed that the hem of her dress had become blackened from the soot on the wooden sidewalk; the color of her tiny shoes was indefinable. Here hand went swiftly to her bonnet.

'Oh please, don't let my new bonnet be soiled!'

A few people were out, either inspecting the devastation or on their way to church. Each one showed their eminent sorrow in their countenance and quiet conversation.

'Hello Mrs. McLean." An elderly lady approached Elizabeth.

Eliz continued, "Isn't this just awful?"

"Worst thing I have ever seen and I've seen a plenty. I just hate those Yankee devils. Just you wait till the boys get home. We'll get 'em."

"I sure do hope so Mrs. McLean." She continued her walk.

It was difficult to remember her city the way it was compared to what it now was. Even as she walked closer to the church, bitter burning hate filled her heart toward the Yankee army that had torched her city. She had never been as given to such feelings of anger and hate as she was now.

She thought of John McIntire who had lost his life while trying to defend his own farm while the Yankee soldiers took all the food and livestock they had. He was surely a brave man, but he and his sons were vastly out numbered. This fact was a tremendous worry for Elizabeth. John had made his decision not to enter the fighting because of strong religious convictions. There were many stories of bravery during the senseless assaults on the passive citizens of South Carolina and the pillaging of their property. Many slaves gave witness to the ruthless behavior of the invaders. Many of them left the state, but the majority chose to stay and help the people whom they had grown to love and considered family. One of these slaves was Zebulon Torrey of Tevah plantation in Mississippi where Elizabeth's cousins lived. He had taken the last name of the master of the plantation and was completely devoted to the Torrey family. He even enlisted in the Rebel army when the war broke out.

Zeb, as he was lovingly called by the family, grew up on the grounds of Tevah where he was taught the Scriptures and to read and write along with the other children. Mrs. Torrey felt very strongly about education for all the children. Elizabeth sat down on a bench in front of the church to wait for Charlotte. In an attempt to occupy her mind with more pleasant thoughts than the destruction around her, she let her mind wander back to Tevah and the story her Mississippi cousins had told her about Zeb.

It was a beautiful Sunday morning, as the story unfolded, under the big oak and beside the twelve neatly painted cabins, each named for one of the Disciples of Christ. Only one was unoccupied, the one called Judas. The praise of the people who attended the service was loud and joyous.

Zeb would say, "Nothin' wrong with bein' excited 'bout praisin' the Lord wif some energy."

The singing was glorious. No musical instrument accompanied the singers as their songs traveled skyward and across the vast cotton fields, in perfect harmony.

Elizabeth's cousin would tell her the sweet story of Zeb and his love, Simmy, and how she sat beside Zeb, at a respectful distance of course. After the altar call, they all made their way to an enormous table where everyone had placed their very best dish. Fried chicken was the most sought after dish and normally was the first thing to disappear.

"Come on Simmy, 'fo you miss out." Zeb would say.

In her gently worn white Sunday shoes, which must have been a size too small, Simmy seemed to tower above Zeb.

Elizabeth smiled to herself at her mental picture of Simmy, toes curled slightly in her shoes and bending her knees just enough so as not to expose Zeb's short stature. She could see a light colored Negro girl, about her own age, with her black hair tied in the back and rolled neatly into a bun. Anna had told her cousin that Simmy was tall and very thin, not the most beautiful of the Negro girls living on the plantation, but definitely the one with the kindest heart. No doubt it was true love for both of them and their destiny seemed to be set.

Like coming out of a fog, Elizabeth looked and the present still surrounded her. She wondered how well her kin in

Mississippi and Tevah had faired. She wondered about the rolling cotton fields all green before the bowls burst open to reveal their bright, snow-white crowns. The enormous oak trees spreading their limbs like giants reaching out to catch some unsuspecting bird flying by too closely. Her thoughts were once again interrupted by Charlotte's high pitched voice.

"Mary Elizabeth, here I am."

There she was hurrying down the dirty walkway as quickly as her short legs would let her travel. She was fourteen, one year older than Elizabeth, but several inches shorter. Her red hair was the color of shiny copper and even more tightly curled than Elizabeth's. They met with a hug and Charlotte began the conversation.

"Isn't it just too awful, our town I mean? I can hardly believe what I've seen." She continued, "Just look at my shoes! Somebody needs to at least sweep the walk away."

The conversation was fast and full of excitement and animation as Charlotte put her hands on her hips in disgust.

"John McLaurin's house barely escaped being burned down completely! His family was lucky that no one was killed."

Charlotte's eyes were wide as she related the McLaurin family's brush with death.

'Blamed Yankees!" Mary Elizabeth was beginning to feel justified in using the term now and recited it as if it were one word.

Charlotte gasped, "Mary Elizabeth, your Papa would skin you alive if he heard you say that, and right in front of the church too."

"I don't care. I truly do hate them. Did I tell you that I prayed for my Mama to become a Confederate spy during the war?"

"No!"

"Well I did but its good she didn't because she never could keep a secret. She told me Mrs. Neeley's cow was having a calf and she let me watch. That's because I begged her to tell me how Mrs. Warren got that baby out of her stomach. I could tell you stuff you wouldn't believe."

"Tell it Elizabeth!"

Elizabeth shook her head in an omniscient fashion, but by days end, Charlotte would know all the gory details of the birthing of a calf, with a few ideas of Elizabeth's own thrown in for effect.

People began to arrive at the church for the very first service since the surrender, each soul ready to offer thanks for being spared or to ask the Lord for help to recover from the loss of property, but most of all for comfort in the loss of loved ones.

"Good morning, Charlotte." Elizabeth's Papa was a very caring and polite soul and his smiling eyes and mild manner made everyone love him.

Papa smiled down at Charlotte and continued, "Your red hair shines like the sun." He took Elizabeth's hand, "Let's go inside and give God thanks for what we have.

Elizabeth hung her head slightly under the pious gaze of her Papa and was feeling a bit guilty for using profanity in her description of the Yankees, but not for her anger with them. Walking into the church that morning Elizabeth noticed a different mood. The people were usually chatting softly and enjoying the company of people they had not seen for a while, but this morning, the mood was very somber. Although the sun steamed in through the beautiful stained glass windows, it was cool inside the church. Every head was bowed as though the whole congregation was asking God for something or perhaps for an answer to the devastation.

The preacher arrived in his black robe, Bible clutched to his chest, and with a solemn look on his face.

He began, "Today we will talk about the meaning of the prayer our Lord gave to the disciples, and through them, to us, on how to pray. In particular, "Forgive us our debts as we forgive our debtors."

"Oh, my stars!" Elizabeth almost had a conniption fit.

She looked down the pew on the other side of the aisle to see Charlotte, whose red curls bobbed up and down as she shook her head back and forth in agreement.

Elizabeth frowned at her and whispered softly, "You little traitor!"

'Red heads are completely unpredictable. Wish I had been a spy or a soldier or something in the war. Blamed Yankees!'

She looked up at Papa to make sure he had not read her mind. Feeling certain that he had not heard her thoughts, she bowed her head reverently and asked God to forgive her for the cursing because she was certain that God had heard.

CHAPTER 2

On Monday morning, Elizabeth woke up with a throbbing toothache. She looked into the mirror and glared at her reflection in utter horror.

"Oh my stars, I look like a chipmunk with a whole winter's store of food in my cheek! Mama, Mama!"

It was a cry of anguish and Mama knew that something was indeed not right. "What in tarnation is wrong with you Mary Elizabeth?"

"My whole mouth hurts, Mama."

"Let me look, honey."

Elizabeth opened her mouth as far as she could for her Mama to get a good look at the problem.

"Well, your gums are swollen. We just need to go to the dentist and let him have a look."

With a worried look toward her mother, pleading eyes and a quivering lip, Elizabeth questioned her.

"What will he do?"

"He may have to just pull it out of there."

"Noooooo," squealed Elizabeth. "I can't even think about such an awful thing!" "Don't be such a cry baby Mary Elizabeth. He has medications that are made to numb the pain."

"I heard that they just crack you in the head to knock you out and then dig out your tooth with pullicans."

"Mary Elizabeth, I don't want to hear all of that nonsense."

She knew that her Mama had been so impressed with the doctor's knowledge that she had nick named him 'the Pope of Dentistry."

That afternoon Mama and Elizabeth made their way to the office of the Pope of Dentistry. They walked inside the neat little office downtown and were met by a very nice looking young man.

"Good morning," he smiled as he greeted them. Elizabeth noticed his perfect teeth.

"Old sugar bug didn't get him I guess," she mumbled.

Elizabeth was smitten right away, all the way up to the time he told her that she was pretty as a speckled pup.

"A pup? A pup? Isn't that a dog?"

The good doctor Neal obviously had not had too many dealings with thirteen year olds. Never the less, Elizabeth crawled up into the chair and opened her mouth. Dr. Neal looked into the chasm.

"Hmmmm, you have a really bad tooth in there," the doctor replied.

Rolling her eyes, Elizabeth kept her mouth wide open so she would not be tempted to bite him.

"What do you think Elizabeth? Should we pull it out of there?"

All Elizabeth could think of was, "If you're the Pope of Dentistry you ought to know what to do with it!"

Patients like Elizabeth could account for part of the reason Dentistry was neither a popular nor profitable profession of the time. Some people were too poor to pay for services and gave the dentist chickens or eggs for his services.

"I'm a little uneasy in this chair, Dr. Neal."

"Well, let's just lean you back a little. What's your very favorite thing Elizabeth?"

"I guess that would be my best friend Charlotte, although she does aggravate me on occasion, but my very worst thing in the world is Yankees. Actually, I feel a little bit sorry for the Yankees myself."

"What in the world for?"

"They had to march around with their jaws all poked out because they didn't have any dentists to take care of their teeth. Did you know our Confederate boys had a Dental Corp?"

"Were you the Pope in charge of them Dr. Neal?"

"No, not exactly. I did serve in the corp but I just plugged and pulled a lot of teeth."

"Does it hurt, the pulling part I mean?"

"Why you can sniff a little anesthetic we call ether and you'll be fine."

After explaining to the doctor that her Mama would not be paying for his services with chickens or eggs, Elizabeth began to relax from her ether. In no time the tooth was out and Elizabeth had made a new friend: The Pope of Dentistry himself.

On the way home, Elizabeth told her mother that she couldn't wait to tell Charlotte about the dentist and show her the tooth.

"Mama, am I a bad person for being happy the Yankees didn't have a Dental Corp and a Pope of Dentistry in their army?"

"I don't think that's a sin Elizabeth, it's the way you feel, but your feelings tend to dictate the way you act. We need to learn tolerance and forgiveness."

"Oh my stars, here we go again. Blamed Yankees! I think when I grow up I'll be a dentist and pull out all their teeth", Elizabeth boiled under her breath.

"Elizabeth, are you listening?"

"Yes mam."

CHAPTER 3

On the morning after her tooth extraction, Elizabeth woke with a little soreness in her mouth. Using her tongue, she explored the empty hole in her mouth.

"Mama, my mouth is kind of sore."

"I'll get the alum and it will be just fine."

Knowing that Charlotte would be bouncing in before she could even get dressed, she crawled out of bed and slipped into a cool little gingham dress.

"What a dream I had last night! Strangest one I've ever had. I guess my mouth was bothering me."

"Good morning." Charlotte bounded into the room with Mama following close behind with the alum.

"Charlotte, I had a real nightmare last night."

"Tell it Elizabeth!"

"Well, it all started with me walking in the woods. The air was all full of smoke and loud noises like cannons being shot. It was like walking inside a cloud or something. Then, in the midst of all that shooting, I saw men running toward me, smacking their lips."

Mama had laid the alum aside.

"Good heavens Elizabeth!"

"Well, the reason I noticed the smacking was because none of them had any teeth."

"Don't you think that maybe that dream was a result of your visit to Dr. Neil's office yesterday?"

"Oh I know what it was." Charlotte was eager to be the interpreter of Elizabeth's dream.

"Don't you remember, Elizabeth? You said you wanted to be a dentist and pull out all the Yankee's teeth."

"Mary Elizabeth Buie, What a terrible thing to say."

With that, Mama placed the alum on the nightstand and walked toward the kitchen.

Elizabeth rolled her eyes.

"I swear Charlotte Royal Gasson, you tell everything you know and make up the rest. Why did you tell that in front of Mama?"

"I didn't think it was so bad."

"You know Charlotte, if my name was Charlotte Royale Gasson, I don't think I'd be telling secrets. Anybody named for a street in New Orleans, in the French Quarter, could be black mailed."

"Whatever do you mean by that Mary Elizabeth Buie? Royale just happens to be a family name."

With that announcement, Charlotte whirled and left the room in a huff.

Turning around briefly she announced that she would never speak to Elizabeth again, "as long as I live!"

"Pooh, she'll be back tomorrow."

Picking up the little tin of alum, she sat down on her bed to recall her dream. "Maybe Charlotte was right and if she was, I'll have to apologize for making fun of her middle name. Ugh, how can I apologize to Charlotte?"

Elizabeth looked outside at the brand new day that had

never been used before. She imagined how she might use it, but in almost every plan, Charlotte was there with her.

"I guess the first thing that I should do today is to go and apologize to Charlotte."

Her mouth didn't seem to hurt any more and the thought of the taste of that alum made her place it back on the nightstand and head for Charlotte's house down the street.

Charlotte's house was a neat, narrow cottage, which reminded Elizabeth of one of the boxcars behind a train. The door was never locked and Elizabeth opened the door.

"Charlotte, where are you? I have something to tell you."

The shiny red hair peeped around the corner of the door leading to the kitchen.

"Tell it Elizabeth!"

Two good friends should never carry grudges and in that instant all was forgotten and additionally forgiven.

"I think you were right Charlotte, about my dream and the trip to the dentist." "Do you really?" Charlotte smiled and the two sat down at the kitchen to discuss the possibilities for the day.

Elizabeth placed her elbow on the table and rested her chin in her hand.

"You know, I can't even remember a time when we were not friends Charlotte Royale."

"Oh Elizabeth, don't call me that."

"Why?"

"Well, she replied, 'mostly the only time I hear it is when my Mama gets mad with me for something I've done and I know that I'm in trouble."

Elizabeth laughter, "Oh that's the same for me too."

Charlotte pulled out her collection of paper dolls that had been pain stakenly cut from a picture catalogue and gave Elizabeth first choice.

"I know I don' want Sally 'cause she doesn't have but one leg and Annie has one arm half torn off."

"Oh Elizabeth, let's go out to the garden. The corn is just beginning to silk and we can get a doll off the corn."

"Good idea!"

They jumped to their feet and headed for Mr. Gasson's garden.

"Any snakes in there Charlotte? You know how I hate snakes."

"No. No snakes. Why do you hate snakes so much Elizabeth?"

Elizabeth rolled her eyes. "Ah, they bite and the devil was a snake once you know."

"Well, he's not now."

"How do you know for sure, Charlotte? They are so sneaky and you know yourself they hide and jump out and bite you when you don't expect it." Elizabeth realized that she had found an ideal spot for one of her stories. In hushed tone, she began.

"One day when God Adam and Eve, Eve was walking in the garden just like we are in your Papa's garden, and Eve heard a soft voice. She looked to see where the voice was coming from and there he was, stretched out on the limb of one of the trees."

"There who was Elizabeth?"

"The devil, Charlotte, only he didn't look like he was the devil. He was very sneaky, all different colors and smiling. He said hello to Eve and told her how beautiful she looked. I told you he was sneaky didn't I?"

Charlotte's eyes were wide with wonder, as she had been taken in with Elizabeth's tale of the snake and the devil.

"What happened then? Tell it Elizabeth!"

"Well, the old snake told her that he sure would like to have something to eat and that he had just passed by a tree in the middle of the garden that had the prettiest fruit growing on it. He wanted to know if Eve had tasted it 'cause he would bet it was the sweetest fruit in the whole place."

"Elizabeth, I never knew a snake could talk."

"Well, this one could and he told Eve to take a little taste 'cause he had pulled a piece of the fruit for her to try."

Charlotte gasped and Elizabeth was really feeling the power of her story telling. "Eve said that God told her she would die if she ate the fruit, but the devil said no she would not. Well, the old devil talked Eve into disobeying God and she ate it and gave some to Adam. All the people blamed Adam and he blamed Eve, but I blame the old devil. Now do you know why I hate snakes?"

Charlotte could not answer and began to back out of the garden, looking around as she left.

"Hey, we not getting any corn dolls in here?" Elizabeth was determined not to leave without the corn and picking two ears as she carefully headed for the safety of the yard, Elizabeth called to Charlotte, "Here, I got two corn babies. You pick yours first."

The two went to the giant oak in the back yard to play with the corn babies. They rode them around on magnolia leaf buggies and made them beds on the soft green moss that grew around the base of the tree.

"Do you think it would be fun to ride around all day in buggies, dressed in fancy dresses and have a lovely white parasol to keep you cool? Everyone would look at you go by and say that you must be a princess. Then at night go to sleep in a nice soft bed with all your servants around to fan you while you slept." The girls played with their corn babies until the silk hair began to fall out and the buggies broke down.

"I'm tired of the corn babies Charlotte, and besides I need to get home for dinner. Mama said that she would make me some chicken and dumplings today. You want to come?"

Tossing their disheveled corn babies aside, they ran inside to ask Charlotte's Mama's permission to go home and dine with her friend Elizabeth.

As they walked to Elizabeth's house, the two chatted gaily. Elizabeth felt obliged to tell her friend about their lunch. She began.

"You remember when we would go out into the back of my house to play and we couldn't even sit down without that big old rooster chasing us away and trying to peck us?"

"Yes."

"Well, he won't be doing that any more. Mama wrung his neck and he will be on the table today with the dumplings!"

They both laughed as they walked hand in hand.

The girls would remain friends through the years to come and each year would be the same with their friendship. The staying power of that friendship made each life more special and complete.

"Race you!" Elizabeth ran ahead.

"Wait up!" Charlotte squealed.

CHAPTER 4

*A*fter the war, the years seemed to roll by in rapid succession. The day for which the two friends had waited with impending dread had at last arrived.

Charlotte would be graduating and going away to college, leaving Elizabeth alone with only the memories of their times together.

The day arrived and Elizabeth hurried to Charlotte's house intent on seeing her childhood friend off at the train station. Reaching her house she called, "Charlotte, come on out or you'll be late for the train."

Hearing no response, panic set in and Elizabeth realized that the family had already left for the station.

"If I don't get to tell her good-bye, I'll just die!"

Elizabeth ran as fast as she could in her long dress. She was determined to see Charlotte before she left.

Nearing the station, Elizabeth heard the call of the Charlotte bird. "Hurry Elizabeth! Did you over sleep on my last day at home?"

"No, I think someone must have given me the wrong time for the departure." The two ran together in a hug that was much akin to one that would resemble a loved one who had been returning home after a very long absence.

"I would have just died if I had missed you!"

Elizabeth looked at her friend with eyes beginning to puddle just before big alligator tears began to fall.

"I had to tell you something dear friend."

Looking up with her sweetest smile, she blurted out, "Tell it, Elizabeth!"

The tears fell as Elizabeth poured out her heart about how very special their friendship was and how much she would miss her. Somehow reality had hit Elizabeth and she was, perhaps for the very first time, understanding what losing something dear actually meant.

Somehow Elizabeth felt a deep loss.

"I'll come home for holidays and things Elizabeth."

Elizabeth shook her head in agreement but suspected that things would never be quite the same.

The shrill whistle of the train could be heard as it came around 'dead man's curve." The smoke from its stack seemed to hang in the air. The big powerful machine neared the station platform and Charlotte tried to hold her curly red hair in place as the steam spewed out like and angry giant.

"Wow, I don't think we were ever brave enough to get this close to the train and now you will be riding on it."

Charlotte told her parents good-bye and then turned to Elizabeth.

"You can write to me and I will answer. You tell me what you are doing and I'll do the same. We will be seeing each other before you know it."

The call startled Elizabeth. "All aboard."

The conductor took Charlotte's two bags and helped her on the train.

"Miss you will have to take your seat before the train pulls out of the station." Charlotte made her way to her seat and sat where she would be able to see Elizabeth as the train left.

Elizabeth had brought a little hanky to brush off any soot that may get on her dress but she noticed that now it was a bit too wet for that. The train began to pull away from the station and Elizabeth observed Charlotte's child-like face as she beamed back at her friend.

The engine spewed steam and cinders as it picked up speed, but Elizabeth did not move from her spot until it had disappeared out of her sight.

She had such an empty, sad feeling inside, almost as though someone had died. Elizabeth shook her head back and forth to break the trance into which she had entered.

"What a baby you are Elizabeth Buie, to think you will never see Charlotte again or that you will never have another friend."

Elizabeth was silently chastising herself.

The walk home seemed longer than usual today as she walked slowly past Charlotte's odd shaped house. The fact that Charlotte was not there anymore returned her to her former state of loss.

"I remember this old walkway when it was covered with dirt and smut from the war and then when we had that gully washer and it was made clean by the rain. I remember when it was covered with snow and Charlotte and I got pieces of tin from the old shed and slid down the steepest part of the walk. With all that it's still here.

Elizabeth sat down on the little bench in front of her house and dug her soggy hanky out of her pocket.

"Memories are so special and that's really the only thing that is lasting." She stood up. "Heavens. Even this old walkway won't be here forever. One day someone will say, what ever happened to that old walk that used to be here and somebody else will say, "Oh it died.'"

Elizabeth began to chuckle at her own analogy of the mortality of the wooden walkway. Things were better. Things always get better if you can find something to smile or laugh about.

"Goodness knows," she thought, "Charlotte Royale Gasson always made my own life a lot more fun."

She walked inside and passed her mother who was washing breakfast dishes. "Did you see Charlotte off this morning dear?"

"Yes mam. She sure looked small sitting on that big old, dirty train."

"I do hope she enjoys college life." Mama always tried to look on the bright side of everything.

Elizabeth wanted to say, "Well, I don't hope she enjoys it. I hope she hates it so much that she will cry and her Mama will let her come home."

Elizabeth!" Mama looked a bit displeased. "Where is your mind? Didn't you hear me? I asked you to help me put these dishes away."

"I'm sorry Mama. I was just thinking about Charlotte and how I'll miss her."

"She'll be home before you know it, dear, and you two will take up right where you left off."

Silently Elizabeth was saying that she didn't really believe that her Mama understood how much they loved each other.

"I know Mama, but what will I do for a friend till she gets home again?"

"This town isn't very big, but there are lots of nice boys and girls here and you should not have any trouble finding another friend like Charlotte."

"Mama, we have been friends all our lives and you don't find friends like Charlotte every day."

"I understand that you feel that way now Elizabeth, but time will pass and you will see all the possibilities."

Elizabeth smiled to herself, "Now there's something funny, so why am I not laughing?"

Everything seemed to remind her of Charlotte.

"Well, I guess I need to look for a new friend. That's funny, where do I start?" Elizabeth had decided to walk down by the schoolyard and have a look around before school started for the year.

"My last year." She thought. "Can't wait to see what wonderful adventures I will have as I go through life alone. Goodness, I'm being so dramatic. Maybe I really ought to get right down to it and try and enjoy my last year of high school."

After a lunch of thinly sliced ham and tomato on bread, lathered liberally with mayonnaise and a small bowl of chilled fruit, Elizabeth gathered her courage and headed for the high school where the kids all gathered. No one was there, today and secretly Elizabeth was strangely relieved.

"Just one friendly old dog," Elizabeth said aloud. "Must be my lucky day."

Two weeks passed and at last a letter came from Charlotte. It was a rather short letter, which left Elizabeth very disappointed. She had expected a long, newsy letter expressing, most of all, how much she missed Elizabeth. The letter talked about her classes and all the cute fellows she had seen on the campus. She couldn't wait to see Elizabeth and she planned on being home at Christmas time. Time was precious because of her class schedule and studies. They would sit down and talk about everything at Christmas.

"Well," Elizabeth thought. "You would think she would be a bit more personal with her comments. I don't care about your schedule Charlotte, I want to hear about you."

Throwing the letter down on the bed, she got up to help Mama with dinner.

"Charlotte Royale Gasson, just you don't hold your breath till I respond to this little note."

The next day, Elizabeth was sitting in Papa's desk, pen in hand and writing to Charlotte.

"Hum'" she thought, "I don't know what to write about either. Perhaps I was too hasty in judging the contents of Charlotte's letter."

Three weeks passed before another letter arrived from Charlotte. This was a great deal newsier than the first, as a matter of fact, it contained information that seemed to be completely out of character for Charlotte. She had a beau!

"Oh my stars!" was Elizabeth's reaction. "I absolutely can not believe this."

She wondered, "What kind of boy would Charlotte be attracted to, or better yet, what kind of boy would be attracted to Charlotte?"

Charlotte was pretty and fun, but Elizabeth never knew that she even considered boys a part of the human race.

"Well, I guess I'll have to listen to all that drivel at Christmas. I hope she doesn't bring him home with her. Oh Charlotte Royale Gasson, you wouldn't dare!"

CHAPTER 5

*I*t was the day of Charlotte's homecoming and Elizabeth was beyond excited. The clouds had been assembling all day and the air had turned cold with the wind picking up strength. Little white flakes had begun to fall like microscopic confetti falling from the sky.

"Snow!" Elizabeth shouted to her mother who was smiling. She had already seen the snow, but wanted Elizabeth to discover it for herself.

"Today is turning out to be quite special for you, dear."

"Charlotte arrives tomorrow Mama, are you making Jesus cookies?"

"You know that I make Jesus cookies every Easter and Every Christmas. I do believe its Christmas time, isn't it?"

Jesus cookies were dainty little margarine treats that were empty inside when someone took a bite.

"Just like the empty tomb of Jesus when He rose on Easter morning." Mama would always recap the story when she made the Jesus cookies. "It's such an important part of our lives." She would say to Elizabeth.

The most difficult part of the process was beating the egg whites to the proper consistency with her little rotary beater. They were made of egg whites, sugar and a little bit of vanilla, but had proved to be a big treat for all the children. Charlotte especially looked forward to the sweet treats each year and would always arrive at the Buie home early on Christmas day.

Elizabeth addressed her mother, "Remember when Charlotte used to come over and just hang around the kitchen waiting for you to bring out the Jesus cookies?"

"Oh yes, I remember. We'll try not to disappoint her this year. I'll make them tonight."

Elizabeth sat in the window seat watching the snow become thicker with each passing minute and as the time passed her excitement grew.

Elizabeth awoke to a world of white. The snow covered everything like a giant quilt.

Hurrying into the kitchen, Elizabeth noticed the dainty little Jesus cookies placed in an orderly fashion on Mama's best Christmas plate. The cookies were arranged so as not to cover all the lovely red flowers bordering the white plate. Elizabeth hugged her mother with a cheery, "Merry Christmas, the Jesus cookies look wonderful and I know Charlotte is going to be one happy visitor."

"What time does her train arrive Elizabeth?"

"I think it's 10 o'clock. I need to get ready to meet it. I just hate to get out and disturb the snow. There's not a mark of any kind in it."

Elizabeth left the house early for the train station. She couldn't help but compare the walkway now covered with the beautiful white, gleaming snow to the day she walked on it just after all the fighting. The old walkway had seen many changes and yet it still remained underneath the devastation and the beautiful snow that now hid the soot of war.

She didn't like to think about all that on this special day.

All she wanted to do was think about Charlotte and how they would sit and talk for hours, the way they had when they played with the corn babies under the oak in the back yard of Charlotte's house.

Elizabeth quickened her pace as she heard the train whistle in the distance. Her heart was racing as she caught sight of the engine and the long plumes of black smoke making their way skyward. They seemed to hover closer to the ground on this cold December day. The train arrived at the station just as Elizabeth stepped onto the platform.

"Good morning, Elizabeth." Charlotte's mother and father were standing all bundled up against the cold. "She's finally home."

"Yes, Mrs. Gasson, I have missed her so very much."

With a great screeching noise, the train stopped and the conductor stepped from the train with a little square step tool for the travelers.

Elizabeth's excitement was elevated, "There she is!"

Stepping down, with the aid of the conductor, Charlotte was smiling as she departed.

"Elizabeth!" she shouted.

She acknowledged her parents with warm hugs and then, after happy greetings and short conversation, motioned Elizabeth closer to the family.

"Elizabeth, please tell me that we have Jesus cookies."

"We have Jesus cookies."

"I have to go home first and spend a little time with my Mama and Papa, but then I'll come to your house and we can visit. I have so much that I want to tell you."

They walked together to Charlotte's house where they said goodbye for a while and Elizabeth proceeded to her own house. Elizabeth burst into the house.

"Mama, put the Jesus cookies out, Charlotte Royale Gasson

is home from the hills. She has to spend a little time with her parents first."

"Well, I should hope so."

"She won't be far behind though because she has a lot to tell me. I especially want to hear about her beau. Bet he's got red hair and wears those thick old glasses."

"Elizabeth, did that sound like a nice thing to say? You know that Charlotte has red hair and it's perfectly beautiful."

"I know Mama, but I think two red heads in the same space might be a little bit too much."

"First of all Elizabeth, you have no idea what Charlotte's beau looks like and second, it's really of no concern to you what kind of beau Charlotte has."

"Yes mam."

The familiar high-pitched voice floated into the kitchen.

"Where are the Jesus cookies? I need Jesus cookies!"

Jumping up from her chair, Elizabeth ran to greet Charlotte again.

"What took you so long? I've been waiting for you for an hour."

"Had to spend time with my Mama and Papa and unpack my clothes."

"Ok, I'll just get a few."

The girls settled down in Elizabeth's room on the bed. The conversation was all over the place until Elizabeth decided to ask Charlotte about her beau.

"What's he look like Charlotte?"

"Well, he's just the cutest thing. He has dark hair and brown eyes."

"Does he wear glasses? Is he blind as a bat?"

"Elizabeth, what in the world prompted you to ask that? No. He isn't blind as a bat. He has lovely brown eyes!"

"Oh." Elizabeth seemed a bit disappointed.

"His name is Matthew and he has all kinds of manners. He holds my hand when we walk and when we cross the street."

"So he's a perfect gentleman I guess."

"Yes, yes Elizabeth, he surely is and he's from Mississippi."

"Is that supposed to explain his good manners?

"Well, his mama did raise him right."

Elizabeth had heard all she wanted to hear about Charlotte's beau. He was not red headed and did not wear thick glasses for his exceptionally poor eyesight.

Hoping to discredit Charlotte's new beau, Elizabeth asked, "What did ole Matthew give you for Christmas, if anything."

Charlotte reached for the dainty chain hidden beneath the yoke of her blouse and produced a tiny gold locket.

"It's kind of small Charlotte."

Elizabeth was a bit disappointed. She had struck out again.

"OK I say we go outside and walk in the snow. I haven't told you all about Matthew yet."

"A little bird told me that I don't need to hear anymore right now."

"What's wrong with you Elizabeth?"

"Nothing, I just don't want to take up all our time discussing people I don't even know."

Sensing Elizabeth's uneasy mod, Charlotte popped a whole Jesus cookie into her mouth and look quizzically at Elizabeth.

"I don't understand your feelings about Matthew. You have never even met him."

"Look Charlotte, for all these years it's been Elizabeth and Charlotte and now it seems to be Elizabeth, Matthew and Charlotte. I guess I see him as sort of a wedge between you and me and it makes me sad."

"Elizabeth, there will never be a wedge between us and our special friendship. Some day you will find a Matthew but we will now and always be friends."

"I really hope you are right, but I can't see myself in such a vulnerable situation."

"That's not my situation Elizabeth. Matthew likes me and I like him."

"Well, that's just peachy. Let's go outside. Grab your coat and let's get out in the snow."

Anxious to see Elizabeth's mood change, Charlotte grabbed her coat and scarf and ran for the door.

"I'll race you!"

Once again it was only Elizabeth and Charlotte, no worries. Only the beautiful white gift from heaven for them to enjoy.

"Hey Charlotte," Elizabeth called.

Charlotte turned to answer her friend and as her reward, she was hit full in the face with a monstrous snowball. She brushed the snow from her face.

"Now you have done it Mary Elizabeth Buie. Prepare for all out war!"

Playing as they had done when they were in grade school, they threw snow, made snow angels and generally just enjoyed being in each other's company. No worries about tomorrow. Tomorrow would take care of itself.

CHAPTER 6

*T*he fun time went on for the friends during Christmas until the day before Charlotte's departure to go back to school. Elizabeth went outside to wait for her friend.

"Yoo-Hoo!"

Charlotte was rushing down the walkway.'

"Come on in, Mama has made a new batch of Jesus cookies."

"Oh yum!"

The two went inside and headed straight for the kitchen and the Jesus cookies all neatly arranged on Mrs. Buie's red and white Christmas platter. Taking a few and tucking them into a napkin they made their way down the long hall to Elizabeth's room.

"Let's just sit on my bed by the window where we can see the snow."

Charlotte took one of the cookies from the napkin.

"I can't understand how your Mama does this."

She bit into the delicious treat and the shell crumbled to reveal absolutely nothing inside.

"Why do you call them Jesus cookies anyway Elizabeth?"

"Well, you know the Jews condemned Jesus because He said that He was the Son of God."

Charlotte became very still as though she was listening intently.

"Then they crucified him on the cross and they thought they had killed Him. Well they took Him off the cross and buried Him in a tomb. That didn't keep Him because on Easter Sunday morning, when they went to the tomb, He had risen from the dead and the tomb was empty. The Jesus cookies are the empty tomb where they put the body of Jesus, so they're empty on the inside."

There was a silence from Charlotte as if she were trying to take it all in.

Elizabeth continued, "Mama leaves the cookies in the oven overnight, just like Jesus stayed in the grave for three days. See, that's what it means."

Still no response from Charlotte.

"Well, say something Charlotte."

"Did the disciples believe He was their Messiah?

"Well, yes, He was."

"Elizabeth, I believe in Jesus the teacher, but I thought you knew. I'm Jewish."

Elizabeth was shocked. All these years and she never knew that her best friend was Jewish.

"But you go with me to church."

"Some people around here don't like Jewish people, Elizabeth."

Charlotte laid her cookies on the bed and left Elizabeth's room.

Elizabeth was speechless. She had offended her friend and didn't know how to fix it. No one had ever told her, not that it would matter to Elizabeth that her friend was Jewish.

That afternoon Charlotte left to go back to college without even a goodbye and Elizabeth was devastated. This was something big that she needed to discuss with Mama.

After Elizabeth had composed herself, she went into the kitchen to ask for some advice from Mama.

"It's so hard, Mama," Elizabeth said as she sat down in a chair at the table.

"I can't believe what has happened."

"It will all work out Elizabeth. It may take some time and a good long heart to heart talk, but I'm sure you are willing to take the first step. I think maybe Charlotte was just hurt because she felt you were accusing her or maybe the Jews in particular, for the death of our Lord."

"Mama, she wasn't mad, just hurt. I think if she had been mad, we could have talked our way through it. I can't believe that I lost my best friend over Jesus cookies."

"Don't be so sure of losing Charlotte's friendship just sit down and write her a short letter. See how it goes."

That night Elizabeth sat down at her desk and tried to think of a way to begin her letter to Charlotte.

"Dear Charlotte," she began.

"How are you and how is Matthew?"

She crumpled the paper and threw it to the floor.

"Guess I just need to think about this a little more before I write this letter," she thought.

She waited another day and then another, hoping that Charlotte would send her a note. None came. After a week had gone by with no news from Charlotte, Elizabeth sat down and penned a short note.

"Dear Charlotte,

I guess you hate me because I haven't heard from you. I'm so sorry if I offended you about the Jesus cookies because that was surely not my intent.

Your friend,
Elizabeth"

With a few more impersonal lines and the salutation, the letter was mailed. All she could do now was to wait.

On her way from the post office, she passed Charlotte's house where they had played so many times together. Somehow the house looked empty.

"Hum", thought Elizabeth, "Just like the Jesus cookies."

She walked into the kitchen to find Mama busy preparing lunch.

"Mama, I just came by Charlotte's house and it looks empty. It made me sad."

"Elizabeth, I have been wanting to tell you but couldn't find the right time. The Gassons have moved away to be closer to Charlotte. I'm sorry, I should have told you but wasn't sure how you would handle it."

Elizabeth tightened her grip on depression. All hope seemed to be leaving her until at last, a letter from Charlotte arrived.

Running into the kitchen, waving the letter, she announced that it was from Charlotte. She had not been this happy since Christmas when she and Charlotte had their snow fight.

She smiled as she ripped the letter open and began to read:

"Dear Elizabeth,

It was good to hear from you. I am glad that you and your family are well. I have been plagued with a cold and cough. Otherwise I am fine. The weather here is nice and it's good to have Mama and Papa close at hand.

Yours truly,
Charlotte"

Elizabeth frowned. What kind of a letter was this? It was cold and impersonal and left Elizabeth confused. She dropped the letter to the floor, buried her head in the big fluffy pillow on her bed and sobbed as someone would cry upon hearing of the death of a loved one.

Elizabeth felt as though she had cried for an hour and that she needed to get up, wash her face and try one more time to reach out to Charlotte. She wrote a nice newsy letter to Charlotte, signing it "With love" and mailed it.

"Now Miss Charlotte, let's see what you will do about this one. I have written twice and apologized once. It's your turn again."

She sealed the letter and made her way down the walkway with her heart once more full of hope.

The letter was mailed and now the only thing left for Elizabeth to do was to wait. She waited two weeks; waiting with great anticipation for a reply to come.

None came.

Months went by with no correspondence between the friends. Elizabeth would have given most anything to hear Charlotte say, "Tell it, Elizabeth."

Elizabeth had graduated from high school and was planning for her adventure in college. She had thought about going to the same university as Charlotte, but she wasn't even sure that she was still there. Actually the thought of attending an all-girl college was not too exciting. Normally the girls who went to these schools became teachers and for some reason, this idea did not appeal to Elizabeth. Mama had told her that the school prepared you for being an excellent wife and mother and also taught you proper manners. Elizabeth fancied herself one who already possessed good manners. Her Mama had given her lessons at home as to which fork to use, where the knife rested once it was used and all the etiquette Elizabeth felt that she needed in life. By graduation time she had made up her mind that she did not want any more education and would find a proper job close to home. It was a decision that would be questioned more than once by Elizabeth in the future.

CHAPTER 7

*T*he correspondence between Charlotte and Elizabeth had come to an end after a while and though Elizabeth thought of her friend often, she slowly began to get on with her life. In Charlotte's last letter, she had mentioned some small problems in her life that she was attempting to get straightened out. Elizabeth imagined that it might involve her love life with Matthew but did not know for sure. She thought it would be a good bet. Never the less, Elizabeth had her own fish to fry and began to think that she would live at home for the rest of her life and be an old maid. The job situation was dire. It was very hard for a young lady to find employment sufficient to support separate living quarters and supply her physical essentials.

Today she had an interview with the manager of a newspaper who was in need of a reporter. Although she had never actually written articles of any kind before, she felt sure that she would be able to pull this off.

The newly established local newspaper was housed inside a former grocery store that had been converted into two offices. It was on the same order as Charlotte's house, long and narrow.

"Mercy," Elizabeth thought, "I don't see how they could get two offices and a newspaper press in this little building."

Elizabeth's arrival was announced by the tinkling of a small brass bell above the front door.

Immediately a very handsome young man stood. Smiling at the new arrival, he introduced himself.

"Hello, I'm Scott Gilmore. You must be Mary Elizabeth."

She smiled and extended her hand.

"Yes, I am. Very nice to meet you Mr. Gilmore."

"Oh please. Call me Scott."

Offering her a chair, he waited for her to be seated.

Well at least he gets an 'A' plus in the manners department thought Elizabeth. "Mr. Gilmore, err, Scott, pardon me for saying so, but you look very young to be the owner of a newspaper."

"Oh, I'm not the owner. My father is the actual owner. I am fresh out of college and my father is giving me the opportunity to use the skills I learned at the university. I guess you would call me the manager in charge of hiring. Do you want to write?"

"I would like to, but I can't give you references. I'll be honest, this would be my first job."

"Then we would start out on the same level as far as experience goes."

"They both laughed and Elizabeth felt as though they had a common bond. He was nice but she thought his hair was a little too long. With the fact stated that she had no previous job experience, Scott was at a loss as to where to go from there and the interview turned into a nice little get acquainted session.

"Elizabeth, why don't you come in again tomorrow and I will see what I can do. To tell the truth, you are the only candidate I have had thus far so your chances don't look too dismal."

She left feeling a bit encouraged about the prospects of becoming a reporter for the newspaper.

She had done her homework about the job market in her

hometown and the market was not good. The only two jobs that she could find available were the reporter job and a sales clerk job at 'The Reading Tree". Elizabeth had asked for an interview with the owner of the bookstore. She wanted to get this preliminary work done, expecting to be able to decide which one she would take after meeting the employers. At least she did not lack confidence in herself.

There had not been a specific time set for her interview at the bookstore so she decided to just go there now.

As she walked to the end of the main street to the shop, she was thinking how much she would like to tell Charlotte about her interview with Scott Gilmore. She could just imagine Charlotte saying, "Tell it, Elizabeth!"

Thinking of Charlotte made her melancholy and she knew that she must regain her composure and be alert and eager before reaching her destination.

The shop was not much larger than the parlor in her own home and smelled musty when she walked inside.

A lady, who looked to be about her mother's age, approached and smiled at Elizabeth when she entered. She was slightly shorter than Elizabeth and a little on the portly side. Wire framed glasses hung low on her nose and her hair was tight against her head and wound into a bun in the back. Elizabeth thought it a bit severe, but just the way she expected a librarian to look.

"Good morning, dear, how can I help you?"

"I believe you are expecting me. My name is Elizabeth Buie. Are you Miss Hinton?"

"I'm Mrs. Hinton, dear."

"Oh, I'm sorry."

"Quite all right, dear, most people just automatically assume that librarians are old maids."

Elizabeth felt that her assumptions had, once again, made

her look like an insensitive idiot. "No sense in dwelling on the faux pas, it was gone and hopefully would be forgotten." She thought.

"You absolutely do not look like an old maid."

Mrs. Hinton smiled sweetly, "Why don't we talk. Are you still interested in the clerk job here?"

"Yes Mam."

"It doesn't pay a great deal, but the hours are flexible and if you are a student, they would give you plenty of time to keep up with your studies. Where are you going to school?"

Elizabeth put her hands behind her back and tried very hard not to look embarrassed.

"Actually, Mrs. Hinton, I have decided not to pursue an education past my high school one."

"Oh, I'm sorry to hear that but college is not for everyone."

"No Mam."

"Your duties would include collecting the money for sales when I am away from the store, keeping the shop neat and the books in order. I would expect you to open the shop on occasion and to lock up at days end. You would receive a portion of the revenue taken in at the end of day. I think you would find me quite generous. Now would you be able to start work on Monday?"

Elizabeth's head was spinning. She was not at all sure that she would like working in the bookstore. No customers were currently in the shop so how much money could she possibly collect in a day?

"Mrs. Hinton, if you don't mind, I would really like to discuss this with my parents before I make a commitment."

"Of course dear. You can let me know of your decision by Friday."

Thanking Mrs. Hinton sweetly for the opportunity, Elizabeth left and walked out on to the windy street.

The clouds had moved in while she was in the bookstore and the sky did not look friendly. She noticed a chill in the air.

"I need to hurry or I am going to be caught in the rain."

Once she reached home, the rain had begun to fall lightly.

"Mama, I'm home from my interviews."

Mama came into Elizabeth's room. She seemed to be very excited, a fact that pleased Elizabeth greatly.

"How did it go?"

"The newspaper job sounded pretty good, but I don't have any experience. The manager I talked with is not but three or four years older than I am and he's very nice looking with good manners."

"Mary Elizabeth, are you looking for employment or companionship?"

"Mama, all I said was that he had nice manners. Anyway, at the bookshop, I think I made a big mistake. I called the owner 'Miss' and she was 'Mrs.'"

"Elizabeth, I've told you about assuming things and to think before you speak. Was she offended?"

"I don't think so because she offered me the job before I left."

"That's wonderful. Did you tell her you would take it?"

"I told her that I would need to discuss it with my parents first and to be honest, Mama, I don't think I would make much money."

"Did you get offered the reporter job as well?"

"No, but I was the only one to apply so the odds are good that I will get the job."

"Mary Elizabeth, I know you pretty well and I get the feeling that you were more impressed with the young man than the 'Mrs.'"

"Mama!"

"What's his name?"

"Scott Gilmore. And his daddy's name is Mr. Gilmore."

"You know, I somehow assumed that would be his father's name. Try to recall his father's given name. Your father more than likely knows him."

Elizabeth rolled her eyes when Mama turned her back to leave the room.

Taking off her damp dress she placed it on the chair and reached for her robe. She sat down at her desk and without giving it a second thought, took out paper and pen and commenced to write: "Dear Charlotte," she began.

CHAPTER 8

She was awakened the next morning by an enormous clap of thunder. Elizabeth sat up abruptly in her bed to hear the rain coming down hard and steady. She looked out her window to see streams of water running down the street outside. The wooden walk way had been thoroughly cleaned by the rain.

"Scott didn't give me a specific time to come in so maybe I'll just wait till this rain subsides."

Walking over to her desk, she noticed her unfinished letter to Charlotte.

"What could I have been thinking?" she questioned.

"I don't even know her address, but I'll just bet Mr. Scott Gilmore could help me find her."

Smiling and humming softly, she chose a neat grey skirt and white blouse. It looked quite business like for a young lady of the day. She admired herself in the full-length mirror in her room.

The rain was beginning to slack up slightly and she felt that when she was finished with her final touches, the rain would be over.

She was having some difficulty with the tiny buttons on

her shoes and she wondered if it was nerves because she was planning on accepting the job at the paper or because she would be seeing Scott again.

Elizabeth walked into the hall where a large black umbrella was always stationed like a soldier ready for action. The rain had almost ended but Elizabeth took the umbrella and walked outside.

"What a gray day," she thought, "but it's much cooler than it was yesterday."

Elizabeth found that her thoughts began to leap ahead to Scott and this day when she would accept her very first job.

Standing up to her full height, she took a deep breath and opened the door of the newspaper office.

Scott was working on the printing press in the back. He looked up to see who had entered and seeing Elizabeth, he smiled.

"Good morning."

Elizabeth smiled and looked down at the floor. Scott had smudges of ink on his nose and right check.

"Hello," she responded. "I must have come to the mechanic shop by mistake."

Scott looked at his hands and realized that he must have a very sooty face.

"Oh this is just to impress the customers so that they will think I've been hard at work."

"Well I hope you wouldn't expect your employees to wear the same kind of make-up."

"Of course not. Does this mean that you have decided to accept my offer of a job here?"

"I've been thinking about it, but I need to ask a few questions first."

"Well hurry up because I need help with this machine."

Elizabeth laughed.

She was beginning to feel very comfortable with Scott and she didn't believe that it was supposed to be this way between a boss and an employee.

"We never discussed salary or my duties. How much authority would I have in deciding about subjects for my stories?"

"Well all your columns would have to be approved before going to print."

Elizabeth smiled, "And who would do the approving?"

"Why the Editor or course."

"And who, pray tell, is the Editor of this newspaper?"

"Why me of course."

Elizabeth laughed and sat down at Scott's desk.

"How about salary?"

Elizabeth didn't want to appear too anxious, but wanted to know that she would receive some sort of meager salary.

"You will be paid for each article that you write."

"That sounds fair."

"I want you to come up with a name for your column."

"When do I start?"

"Unless you want to get inky and help me today, tomorrow would be good."

Elizabeth felt as though she was walking on air all the way home. The rain had ended and the sun was out bright and warm. Standing in front of her own front door, Elizabeth paused for a moment and then flung open the door in a rather dramatic fashion. Gathering her scarf across her face to cover her nose and mouth, she stepped into the room and announced:

"I have returned, Mother!"

Anna Buie turned and looked at her daughter in total astonishment.

"What in the world are you doing Elizabeth?"

"Oh Mother," still in character, "I am an employee of the daily newspaper. Would you like to have my autograph?"

"Wonderful! What is your salary and when do you start?"

"I start tomorrow and I don't know exactly what my salary will be yet."

"And you took the job? Elizabeth!"

"I get paid for each article Mama."

"How much for each article?"

"Well, I don't exactly know yet."

"What will you write about?"

"I don't exactly know yet."

"Elizabeth, what do you exactly know?"

Taking the scarf from her face, squinting her eyes and wrinkling up her nose, she began to think that perhaps she had been too quick to accept the offer. It just all seemed to fit when she was talking with Scott at the newspaper office. It isn't as if she had signed a contract for this job. She thought, "Yes, this will be all right because I trust Scott. He seems like such an honest person even though his hair is a little bit longer than normal."

There was so much to consider and she had her first day of her first job in the morning. She had to come up with a name for herself or her articles.

Elizabeth ran to her room, picked up pencil and paper at her desk and began to explore her brain for a name. It would need to be catchy. She thought if she knew what type of article she would be writing that she might be able to come up with a more appropriate name.

She lay down across her bed and closed her eyes in order to concentrate more effectively, but she fell asleep instead. The morning sun streaming through her window onto her pillow awakened her.

"Oh no," Elizabeth sighed as she sprang from her bed and got dressed. "I can't believe I fell asleep."

As she rushed down the street, she struggled with coming up with and excuse for coming to work late on her first day. Out of breath, she reached the newspaper office and walked inside. The little bell jingled merrily. Scott was at his desk working on a story of some sort.

"Good morning, Scott. It's me, the late Elizabeth Buie. Am I fired on my first day for being late?"

Scott laughed. "Actually I don't recall telling you what your hours would be."

"I don't think you did, exactly."

"Well, let's not get bogged down with that. What name did you decide on for your column?"

Elizabeth plopped down in the chair beside Scott's desk.

"I didn't exactly come up with one. You see, I fell asleep while I was working on that. I'm really sorry that I have started out on such a slippery slope. I don't intend to let you down again. I really want to come up with a good name for my articles that I would be expected to write."

"I can understand that. What would you like to write about Elizabeth?"

"Well, I don't want to publish recipes or anything as mundane as that. I really love to write stories about people and I feel I would be pretty good at that."

"Sounds interesting but you would have to be open to any improvement the Editor would deem necessary for the integrity of the story."

"Who would do that? Oh, I know. You would!"

Scott laughed, "Exactly."

"I suppose I could live with that but you have to give me some time to write my stories."

"You would be expected to write one or two a week. They don't need to be long, just entertaining."

Elizabeth squinted her eyes and clinched her teeth as one might at being punched in the stomach.

"What's the problem? Do you think that's too much for you to handle at first?" "Not exactly. I was thinking that some of my stories might be a bit too long and some a bit too short."

"Remember, I told you that you could write what you would like but if you don't come up with a story a wee, we can fill in with home town gossip on the next. That's easy to write about. You know you write about Aunt Claireece visiting with the Tates for the annual family reunion or Karen coming to celebrate one of her crazy brother's birthday."

"That sounds good enough. I can do that."

"I think the one thing you need to take a little time with is finding a name for your stories and a separate one for the articles you write."

"I think you are right."

"Why don't you go home and spend some time thinking about what you are going to write and under what name. Do you have any ideas?"

"Not exactly. In fact this has been a real *Not Exactly* day today. I'll see you tomorrow, on time, and ready to work. By the way, what time do I need to be here? Eight o'clock?"

"Well, not exactly."

Elizabeth grinned and walked toward the door in a much better mood than the one she brought in with her.

CHAPTER 9

Elizabeth had begun her new career as a newspaper woman with excitement and determination. She would be the best reporter ever or so she thought. Her community news column would be called 'Cousin Cloie's Corner' and her story section would be written under the name Hilda W. Roy. Nobody would ever be named Hilda W. Roy. Secure in the knowledge that no one shared her numde plum, she proceeded to write her first story. She found that time was too short to complete a regular story and so she wrote the community news titled "Cousin Cloie's Corner."

Her article began with the garden party that Laura Lee Vaughn had at her house on Saturday and mentioned all who attended, and what they wore. Not very exciting until you got to the paragraph about Herbert Broadaway's sixtieth birthday party out on the river when the pick-up truck jumped into gear and rolled down into the water. People sitting in the bed of the truck, enjoying their beverages, either jumped or rolled to safety before the truck breathed its last gasp and disappeared into the river."

(This article would later draw a few negative comments but for the most part, people would love it.)

"The grass fire at the old Harper home place in the Wilton community seemed to have been started by two boys smoking cross vines and rabbit tobacco. The two boys were not named in the article because their punishment had been carried out by the parents and seemed to be severe enough to fit the crime.

The dinner on the ground at the First Baptist Church had been postponed until next Sunday because of the heavy rain. The Ladies Auxiliary had their monthly meeting in the Salis community. It was hosted by Miss Betty Pender. Next month the meeting will be held at the Methodist Church. Miss Pender has requested that the hostess not bring tomato sandwiches due to the delicate digestive system of some of the members and the inadequate facilities at the church."

Elizabeth was having a grand old time with her articles for the paper and Scott was more than pleased. He was selling more papers than ever before and he attributed that increase to Cousin Cloie's Corner.

"Do you think you might get Ms. Hilda W. Roy geared up and ready for print? Next week seems to be a pretty slow week socially and we need to fill space." "I'll see what I can do, but I really enjoy the community news."

That night Elizabeth sat down at her desk and began to get her creative juices flowing. The best stories, to Elizabeth, were always the ones that she had heard from her family. She took her pen and began to write.

"My grandfather was a hunter and spent a good deal of his time in the woods looking for game to supply his family with food. On this particular hunting trip, it was a cold December day and the edges of the ponds were beginning to ice over. Granddaddy's breath hung heavy in the air and looked like smoke as he breathed out. He stomped his feet as he walked to keep them warm and pretty soon, a little pond came into view.

A young boy, about twelve years of age, was standing at the edge of the water with a small black and white dog in his arms. Granddaddy watched as the boy pulled him out of the water for the second time.

Granddaddy approached the young boy.

"Why are you throwing your dog into the pond son?"

"My dad said that I couldn't keep him and I'd have to get rid of him. I just can't let him die."

Tears began to roll down the ruddy cheeks. The December air was cold and the puppy seemed near death.

"How about I keep the dog for you and you can visit him whenever you want to."

The lad nodded his approval and handed the pup to Granddaddy who tucked the dog inside his heavy hunting jacket and started home.

Once inside the comfort of the warm home, the grateful puppy was revived, wrapped in a soft warm dishtowel and placed beside the glowing fire. The pup, warm and secure, slept beside the warm fire, surrounded by my father and his four other siblings.

Daddy's older brother Kenneth wanted to call him Buster but his youngest sister, Kris, explained that they did not know for sure that it was a boy dog. Katherine, the middle sister, picked up the dog, turned him upside down and then back down.

"Yep, it's a boy all right," she said.

The oldest sister, Kelly, was very excited about a name that she said would be perfect for the puppy.

"We should call him Moses," she said, "because he came out of the water!"

Grandma was not too sure that naming a dog Moses would be proper.

But then Kenneth looked up at his mother and said, "Aw

Mama, God wouldn't mind. Besides, he did get pulled out of the water."

With this, they put the stamp of approval on the dog with the Biblical name. "Moses."

The next week, Elizabeth submitted her story to Scott for his approval.

"Elizabeth, where do you get these stories? I think I've got me a winner. If you keep pumping these gems out, we are really going to increase circulation. I'll have to give you a raise!"

Elizabeth was extremely pleased with Scott's reaction to her story.

"I just tell stories that my daddy has told me. Our family is quite unique."

The next story was a community article by Cousin Cloie's Corner and it was rich.

"In the Homewood Community News, Homer Epps told the sheriff that his prize pig was stolen right out of the pen. He was very much afraid that all the evidence had been eaten up by now, but if it had not, please return the pig and no charges would be filed.

In Silver Creek this week, the church witness team from First Holiness church was shot as by Rufus McIntyre when they approached his farm, in an attempt to get him to visit with them in the church. Rufus said that he thought they were revenuers. No one was hurt in the altercation.

Luther Smith's farm was invaded by a swarm of bees this week. Luther proceeded to scoop them up and was chased from his own garden. He suffered many painful stings."

Elizabeth was into her new job and hoped that she would not run out of stories for a long while. She began to think back into her own childhood and of her friendship with Charlotte. It was the first time that she had thought of Charlotte in many weeks. She also remembered that she wanted to ask Scott to help her find her friend and so she went to him.

"Scott, I have a favor to ask of you. I have a childhood friend who is very special to me and we have gotten out of touch with one another. Is there any possible way that you may be able to locate her?"

"I can try. I do have contacts with different newspapers. It's worth a shop. Do you want me to try?"

"That would be great! I just don't know where to begin."

"Give me first and last name, schools attended, any friends that you may remember her mentioning, thinks like that."

"Sure, I'll ask Mama also. She may know something about the Gasson's that I don't know. There was one big thing that I wish someone had told me and that is that the family is Jewish."

"Elizabeth, that doesn't sound like a Jewish name to me."

"Oh, I don't know. Maybe they didn't want people to know that they were Jewish."

"How did you find out?"

"One day I was talking about the Jesus cookies that Mama makes every year, especially at Easter time and sometimes at Christmas. She asked me what they meant because she ate them every year and was very fond of them. I told her the story of Jesus, His crucifixion, and his resurrection from the tomb on Easter morning. I told her how the cookies were empty just as the tomb was that morning."

"Why did that offend her?"

"I don't know, unless she felt that I was condemning the whole Jewish race for killing Christ."

"We really need to find her," Scott said.

Weeks flew by and Elizabeth continued her assault on the

newspaper business, enjoying every minute, while Scott was working behind the scene in an effort to cover every lead he had as to the whereabouts of Charlotte Gasson.

Elizabeth never questioned him about the progress he was making, if any at all. It seemed to her that too much time had passed and they did not have enough information to go forward. She never truly believed that she would ever see her friend again. Charlotte could be married by this time with a family of her own. It was at this point that Elizabeth remembered the name Matthew.

"Matthew was from Mississippi", she smiled as she remembered that Matthew was from somewhere in Mississippi. She hurried to tell Scott the new information.

Scott was getting the office in order, as much as he could. Seeing Elizabeth walk in, he smiled at her.

"You must really love this place to come to work on Saturday!"

"I just thought of something to tell you about Charlotte. She had a beau. His name was Matthew. He's from Mississippi, somewhere in Mississippi."

Only then did it occur to her what a small thing it was. Mississippi was a rather large area and there must be multiple Matthews in Mississippi.

"I'm sorry," she said. "I don't know what I was thinking."

"Don't be silly. At this point we can use all the information we can get. Who knows, this might be just what we need to track down Miss Charlotte." Elizabeth thought that the world needed more Scotts. He never made her feel dumb no matter what she said.

"We have Charlotte Royal Gasson, a red haired little Jewish girl who attended North Carolina University, and her beau is named Matthew from the state of Mississippi. I think that's a good amount to begin with. If you had not told me where

Matthew lived, we would have missed the whole state of Mississippi."

"You are such a positive human being Scott. That's one reason I like you so much."

"You like me so much Miss Elizabeth? Are you trying to tell me something?" Feeling her face begin to flush, she whirled around, "You Cad! Absolutely not!" And she made a fast exit.

"Where's your sense of humor?"

She could hear Scott chuckle as she slammed the door.

CHAPTER 10

A year had gone by and Elizabeth thought that her story well had just about dried up. When she opened the office door to begin her day, she was thinking about nothing except the next article she would write.

Scott looked up and smiled his infectious grin.

"Can't wait to hear the story you will be telling today."

Elizabeth gave him a half-hearted smile.

"Neither can I."

"What? No story to be told by Hilda W. Roy? That's kind of hard for me to believe."

"I'll come up with something, but it may take a while."

"Just so you do it in time for me to get it in this week's paper. I know some people in this town who would more than likely come up here and lynch me if we don't give them a story."

Scott felt very badly because he had not had the time to spend on looking for Charlotte, but the managing of the paper and all the extra work it required was extremely time consuming.

Elizabeth sat down at her desk, leaned back with her eyes closed and tried to clear her mind.

Scott knew the process, he had seen it before, and it was

Elizabeth's ritual for calling up her memories. Today she seemed to be having difficulties in thinking of anything outside the realm of Charlotte and what she might be doing and where she might be.

She opened her eyes.

"Scott, do you mind if I take a little break and clear my mind? I need to give this article a bit of thought. I need to walk around and get inspired."

Scott chuckled. "Whatever it takes Elizabeth. Just make sure that you come back before dark so I will know Miss Hilda is all right."

"Sure will. I don't plan on it taking too long."

She went out into the street. There were not many citizens out. Elizabeth looked up at the sky at the dark clouds as they began to accumulate overhead. She sat down on a long green bench in the park but not too far to run for shelter if the bottom fell out.

"The sky looks so heavy."

The black clouds seemed to grow and press downward nearer the ground. Almost looks as if the sky is about to fall."

Elizabeth jumped to her feet.

"That's it!"

She hurried back to the office and got inside before the rain started.

"There you are. I was wondering if you'd beat the rain. I should have known you would."

"You know me, don't like to get wet."

Elizabeth quickly sat down at her desk and began to write.

As Scott watched her, he knew to say no more. Hilda W. Roy was on the job.

Elizabeth looked at the title of her new store, "The Day the Sky fell", and continued to write.

We can only imagine what this world was like over 3000 years ago, but we do know that it was at that time that the sky fell. Yes, the sky fell right down on mankind.

It was an early time in the history of man and there were many people living in God's creation. The main problem was that where you have people, you have disobedience and sin. Most of these people had become unbelievably wicked and displeasing to God.

However, there was one man who tried to observe God's law and he was honored by God for his service. Noah had found grace in the eyes of the Lord.

It was God's intention to destroy all the wickedness in the world He had created, but at the same time, save Noah and his family.

God gave Noah the command to build an ark capable of protecting his family and two of every kind of animal. It must have seemed an impossible task for Noah when God gave him the plans for that enormous construction but believing God to be powerful enough to accomplish anything, he began the work. In a land of desert and very little rain, Noah's neighbors laughed and called him a fool.

"He has taken leave of his senses," seemed to be the general opinion as Noah continued his work.

Each day the boat grew larger until it seemed to reach almost to the sky. When the collecting of the animals began, the laughter of the people grew even louder.

"Unbelievable!" the people would say. Staying a safe distance away from the animals, the people continued their ridicule of Noah. After the last animal had been taken on board the ark, Noah's family went inside and God Himself shut the door.

At first only small drops of rain fell on the thirsty, dry land and the people were glad. It would be good for their crops. All the while, the clouds gathered over the land so thickly that they almost shut out the sun's light.

Soon the lightening began to flash, sending crashing sounds of thunder to the earth. The people went inside their tents, still happy to see so much rain. Then, just over the sound of the rain, rumblings under the ground could be heard and felt. Frightened looks were on the faces of Noah's neighbors as the men peeked out from the tents in hopes of seeing higher ground where there was no water.

With a mighty explosion, the earth burst open and water gushed out from deep beneath the surface. Panic ensued as the water continued to rise and screams of frightened people could be heard as they pleaded for Noah to let them into the ark, but God had shut the door. The sky had indeed fallen on a sinful race of people. Surely some would say, "How sad that God would do that. They didn't have a chance." But yes, they did but they didn't obey God. Would He have been just if He had not punished disobedience?

God did leave His promise after that flood, and that's the beauty of a merciful God who gives his people hope. He put His sign in the heavens, a rainbow to tell His people that He would never again destroy the earth with a flood. Now we can look up and know that the sky will not fall again. God's mercy holds it up for us!"

Elizabeth put her pen down and looked at Scott.

"You done?" He asked.

"I guess I am, but you had better read it before you approve it. I'm not so excited about it. Everyone knows the story of Noah and the flood. I may have bombed on this one. Read it and be honest in your opinion. I can always go outside and sit in the rain for inspiration. The dark clouds must have inspired me to write about Noah."

"I'm sure it will be fine. You are your own worst critic."

"I just know when I don't feel good about something I've written."

Scott picked up Elizabeth's story and began to read. Elizabeth, once again, thought about her friend Charlotte. Finishing Elizabeth's latest offering, Scott looked at her.

"Elizabeth, this is a fine story. It's not your best, but there are people out there who may not be familiar with the story of Noah and the flood. Your description of it was very good. I know it scared me, and who knows how this story might affect people. It's like the Jesus cookies and your friend Charlotte. How could that story of the Jesus cookies have impacted her life? You don't know what God's plan is for the stories you write or how they will impact lives. Just let them speak, as long as you write from your heart, and you do."

Scott always had a way of making her feel better and this was no exception. She didn't really understand her own feelings for Scott and surely did not know how he felt about her. There were times, like this one, when she felt all warm and comfortable about him, and the other times when she truly felt she could wring his neck.

"You OK?" She heard Scott's voice and shook her head as she emerged from the trance that had taken control of her body.

"Sure. I was just thinking about, uhhh, Charlotte."

"What a lie," she thought.

"Well, I say we go with the story for this week Miss Hilda, and spend a little time on our search for our illusive, red haired Charlotte. The rain has stopped. Let's go get a bite of lunch. My treat."

"I never turn down free food. Let's go."

Scott locked up the office behind them, not because there was anything of value inside, but it had become a habit.

There was not much conversation as they walked down the

boardwalk. Each one was more or less wrapped up with their own thoughts and concerns.

Stopping at the Dinner Bell, a small diner and boarding house on the corner of Main Street, Scott opened the door for Elizabeth.

"What a gentleman," she thought. "His mama raised him right."

Inside the dining room, all the boarders had assembled at one very large table. The smell of fried chicken, fresh vegetables and coconut cake filled the room. They found two empty chairs and sat down. Grace had already been said over the food and Scott found himself hoping that all the fried chicken was not gone. Elizabeth selected a crispy drumstick from the chicken platter and a variety of fresh vegetables in small amounts. Scott, not being quite so dainty, piled onto his plate, high with chicken, mashed potatoes and gravy and vegetables. Sweet tea was always served at all the meals.

"Goodness Scott, are you hungry? When did you eat last?"

"Well, Miss Elizabeth, I have a big appetite and I do dearly love fried chicken. I don't have anyone to cook me big dinners like this one."

Elizabeth suddenly became uneasy about being able to swallow the mouthful of food she had been chewing.

She felt that she had intruded into Scott's personal space.

"I guess you have done it again," she thought. "Butted into someone else's business that's none of yours."

She realized at that point that she really didn't know much about Scott's like. She had never asked because she did not want him to know that she was that interested, and he had not ever volunteered any information himself. Elizabeth decided she would very tactfully, ask Scott a few questions, but not now. This did not seem to be one of her tactful days. She thought it wise to do that at another time.

Her feelings for Scott were baffling. She could not make up her mind whether or not this was just friendship or perhaps a bit more.

That night Elizabeth climbed into her bed thinking of Charlotte and her job, and yes, of Scott. She wondered what kind of mixed up dream she would have tonight.

CHAPTER 11

*T*he years had gone by quickly for Elizabeth. She was twenty now and had rented a room at Mrs. Tate's boarding house. It was a small room on the second floor, but all she could afford on her salary at the newspaper office. It gave her a feeling of great independence to be on her own, although she lived less than a quarter of a mile from her mother and father.

She had a quaint desk at the end of her bed which was her greatest necessity. She shared an upstairs bathroom with a very lovely young woman whose name she could never seem to recall. It worked out well because of the work hours. Her friend left for work at seven which left the bathroom open for Elizabeth to take a quiet leisurely bath and get ready for her day. The food was quite delicious since Mrs. Tate was an excellent cook. Elizabeth's favorite was her asparagus casserole. In her spare time, which was rare, Elizabeth loved to sit on her bed, look out her window, and scan the old buildings in her town. She thought of all the things that they had endured. The war had taken its toll on some of the brick structures still standing, while most of the wooden framed buildings in the town area had been burned, and had to be rebuilt.

On this particular day, Elizabeth was in one of her trances, as she often was when it occurred to her that she still had a story to write for the paper this week. Deciding not to go into the office today, she sat down at her desk and began her story. This was one that grandfather would tell about grandmother.

"I think I'll call this one, "A Little Bird Told Me.""

She began to write:

As the sun disappeared from the sky, it left a beautiful painting of red, orange and yellow with its exit. It was summer and the air hung heavy with the smell of honey suckle. The figures of three small girls frolicked in the front yard. They could hear the drum of the bullfrogs and the chirping sound made by the crickets to announce the end of day. A tiny voice called out from behind the screened door in the kitchen.

"Come inside," it called again.

Hearing no response, the four year old ventured out into the yard and continued his warning.

"The sun is down and the Booger man is out to get you!"

This prophecy was proceeded by shrill shrieks and the rapid scramble of the three girls for the safety of the house.

Christine, the youngest, had been quite shaken about the thoughts of the booger man.

The four burst into the kitchen, letting the screen door bang shut.

"My stars," their mama said as she moved to pick up a pork chop that had slipped from the platter in all the commotion. With lightning speed, Katherine pounced on the chop that had been lying in a splattering of grease on the kitchen floor.

"Five second rule!" she called out with a mischievous grin.

"Put that thing down," her mother warned. "It's hot besides being dirty."

"I wasn't going to eat that, mama." With her little brother gazing longingly at the greasy morsel, she threw it into the garbage.

"What about the hungry children in China?"

Janice was nine and was very dramatically inclined.

"You think they'd eat that?" Katherine was first in line of the chorus line in favor of letting the chop rest in peace.

"Yeah," Christine was eager to participate.

Mama, on the other hand, felt she should use this even for a lesson of some sort.

She began, "Janice, I'm proud of you for thinking of others and not wanting to be wasteful. I feel sure that was what you were thinking."

Janice smiled, being very pleased with her mama's compliment.

"Yes, mama, that's what I was thinking."

Katherine rolled her eyes, "Well, just get it out of the garbage and wrap it up for China, or better than that, you could let the dog have it. A dog has to eat too." The dog was preferred over China by Katherine.

While the war was raging about the dirty chop and what to do with it, Christine looked with angelic face at the pork chop still perched precariously on a napkin in the garbage. Her chubby little fingers picked it up, and she took a good sized bite from the cleanest looking part. Then she returned the remainder to the garbage.

After all the commotion had subsided, Kenny looked into the garbage to retrieve the meat for the family pet.

"Hey!" he shouted. "Somebody ate a bite of my dog's pork chop!"

"All right, everyone get ready for supper." Mama had ignored the remark. After supper, Christine went to her mother's chair and climbed into her lap.

"Mama," she said looking up with wide bright brown eyes. "Do you know who ate that chop?"

"Yes, I think I do," her mother looked down at her with smiling eyes.

"And I believe I know who spilled the milk on the floor in the kitchen this morning, and who wrote on the table cloth with a little pencil."

"Mama, tell me how you know all this stuff. I know you didn't see it all."

"No, Christine," she said, "I have a special messenger that watches for me."

"Who is it, mama? Who tells you all the secrets?"

"Why, Christine, I thought you knew. A little bird told me."

From that time forward, Christine was very careful of what she did any time birds flew near her house.

She picked up her story and decided to take it in early and perhaps organize her desk a little bit. She seldom got caught up with her work to the point she could do any organizing. When she walked in, Scott smiled his usual big grin.

"How's my favorite reporter today?"

"You mean your only reporter, don't you?"

"You don't know that for sure. If you haven't written me a story for this week's edition, I may be getting another reporter."

"You couldn't make it without me and you know it."

"You may be partly right about that," he smiled.

"Then you need to give me a raise so I can buy some food to eat."

"Oh, all right. I'll compromise. I'll take you out to eat tonight."

"When do we leave?"

Scott grinned, "Right now. Get your coat on because it's beginning to turn cold."

It was December and the snowflakes had just begun to fall in the mountains.

As they walked to the little restaurant, Elizabeth was not aware that she was humming.

"What's that tune you're humming, Elizabeth?"

"I don't even know the name of it. I'll think of it in a little while."

"Well, tell it, Elizabeth!"

Shocked by his response, Elizabeth asked, "Why did you say that?"

"Say what?"

"That's what my Charlotte would always say when she wanted to know what I was thinking."

They walked on in silence and Scott reached for Elizabeth's hand. Not a word was said, but the feeling of belonging to one another was finally there. She was happier than she had been in months, just to know that he thought of her as more than just a friend.

The dinner was memorable as the two sat across from one another and literally gazed into each other's eyes.

"Elizabeth, I want to tell you something that I should have said a long while back. You are the best friend I have ever had and I love you dearly."

"We were so close as friends that I suppose I really didn't know that it was love that I felt for you too."

It was the most beautiful moment that Elizabeth could ever remember having in all her twenty years.

"You need to meet my folks," Elizabeth was so anxious for her parents to see what a fine man Scott was. She thought that he may need to get his hair trimmed a little before he met her dad.

On the walk home, Elizabeth felt she was walking above the ground. It was a night that she did not want to end. They sat down on the long green bench just outside the boarding house and Scott took Elizabeth's hands in his.

"How will we ever get any work done ever again? All I will want to do is just sit and look at you."

He leaned in slowly toward Elizabeth and kissed her very gently, almost as if he thought she would break.

"I love you so very much. I don't have the words to express the depth of my love."

Elizabeth felt the tears sting as they rolled down her face. Wiping them away with his soft glove, he kissed her cheek.

"I have to go inside, Scott. Mrs. Tate might not appreciate our kissing on her bench."

"There are just so many things I want to say to you. I can't believe I've held them in all this time. I was attracted to you that first day you came in for the job interview."

Elizabeth stood and watched Scott rise to face her. This would have to be the one last kiss before she went inside.

"I can hardly bear to leave you," Scott said as he took her hand and walked toward Mrs. Tate's boarding house. True love at last for Elizabeth. Her first kiss from a wonderful man. She floated as she walked past Mrs. Tate.

"You all right, dear? You look different. You are either sick or you are one of the most in love people I ever did see."

"Mrs. Tate, I guess it has to be the last one you said."

She went upstairs to her room and got ready for bed. This was her night to dream and she intended to dream big. No doubt in her mind about the dream she would have tonight and when the sun came up in the morning, she would be headed to the office, hoping against hope, that what she had experienced this night would not be part of her dream. Elizabeth was hopelessly in love.

CHAPTER 12

*L*ife for Elizabeth and Scott seemed to be Utopia. They were talking about wedding plans.

Elizabeth had now met Scott's family. She made a special bond with his sister, Carine Nanette. Elizabeth liked her right away. She was beautiful with the rare ability to make you smile by her very presence when she walked into a room. They talked a great deal of their time about Scott. This was altogether for Elizabeth's information. Elizabeth laughed when Corinne mentioned the possibility of catching him when he was asleep and clipping a little bit of his hair. Elizabeth knew from Scott that his sister had a beautiful singing voice and was an excellent musician. She would ask her to sing and the play the piano for her on any occasion she visited the Gilmore home.

"I hope that our children will be able to sing." Elizabeth did not fancy herself with any musical talent.

"I have never been able to sing."

"You know what, Elizabeth? I have never been able to write a story. I guess God gave us all different talents so that we all wouldn't do the same thing."

Elizabeth smiled, "Makes sense to me."

"Tell me about your friend, Charlotte. Scott says you miss

her and that you two were the best of friends. I can imagine you wanting desperately to have her attend your wedding."

"It would truly be a dream come true, but I don't hold out much hope for that anymore."

"Oh, Elizabeth, you can't give up hope. There has to be a way to locate her. I know you don't have much free time right now, but when you get things worked out with the wedding and everything, maybe you can pick it up again. The good thing is that you have already eliminated some of the leads. The last one may be the one that pays off for you."

"Thanks, Corrine, you make me feel good again about the possibilities."

"I guess I need to get to the office and do a little work or my boss might fire me." "Hey, that's one thing you don't ever have to worry about now."

Elizabeth went back to the office. As the door opened and the little bell announced her, Scott made his way to the door.

Kissing her sweetly on the lips, "Where have you been, my love?" Scott smiled down at her.

"I was visiting with your sweet sister," said Elizabeth.

"Were you two planning strategy on how to jump out when I least expect it and cut off my gorgeous hair?" taunted Scott.

"Have you been eavesdropping?" said Elizabeth. "I thought so."

"I want you to know that I plan on getting my head shaved before the wedding." "Oh, I don't think so, mister!"

She gave Scott a quick peck and went to her desk.

"Don't tell me you don't have an article ready for this week."

"I'm sorry. You see I have this guy who drives me crazy. I love him dearly, but he won't leave me alone and I can't get my work done."

"Oh, I see how it is. I guess I'm going to have to crack down on the help."

"I know that you are smarter than that."

She put her pen aside and squinted as she looked at him.

"You bet I am, Miss Cloie."

Her article for this week would have to be a gossip column. She began to write: "It was quiet this week in the Salis Community, except for the visit of Miss Pender to check on her sister's garden. Miss Betty said that due to the lack of rain she was fearful that it may be in a state of disrepair. While on her errand of charity, Miss Betty tripped on a shovel which had been carelessly dropped and twisted her knee. She was doing fine but will be laid up for a couple of days. Delbert Eady was arrested in town last week on a charge of public drunkenness. He is in the city jail and has requested that no one tell his wife. Please honor Delbert's wishes as Mrs. Delbert has quite a good aim with that rolling pin. I wish to announce my engagement to a very nice boy. In the future, you may see his name in this column, if he misbehaves."

"This will have to do. Fill in with something. I can't think about anything but wedding and how you felt about my parents, honestly."

"You know, I will just come right out and tell you the truth. They were exactly as I expected them to be. They were kind of hospitable and your mama is a peach. She kept wanting to feed me more cake or anything that I wanted. If you are as good a cook as your mama, you won't ever have to worry about being traded in on a newer model."

"Who mentioned a trade in? That's not ever going to be an option, Mr. Gilmore." He walked over and gave her a long, passionate kiss.

"I'm in this for the long haul."

The wedding plans were in full swing now, but a definite time had not been set. Elizabeth thought it would be smart to proceed with some of the details even before the date had been decided.

"I have invitations to decide on, wedding dress to buy, cake to order, and bride's maids to pick...." She stopped mid-sentence.

"I do so wish I had my Charlotte to be a part of the best day of my life." Elizabeth wandered off track once more and was back in Charlotte's back yard making mud pies and spinning yarns for her most avid fan. She could almost hear Charlotte just before the tale began.

"Tell it, Elizabeth!"

A loud clap of thunder jarred Elizabeth to a state of reality.

"I remember Mr. Gasson's first name! I remember it!"

She jumped to her feet and literally flew down the street toward the office and Scott.

Bursting through the door, she sent the little bell spinning across the floor. "What's wrong, Elizabeth? Is someone hurt or dead or what?"

Oh, I'm sorry, Scott, but I just remembered Charlotte's father's first name. That's good, isn't it?

"Yes, sweetheart, but couldn't you have told me with less flair? I thought the world was coming to an end."

"Scott, you just don't realize how very important this is to me."

"I'm sorry, sweetie, I really do, but you need to do this calmly, don't you think?"

"Don't you even like Charlotte?"

"I don't even know Charlotte, but if you like her, I'm quite sure I will like her too."

Elizabeth closed her eyes and tucked her chin all the way to her chest. With a huge sigh, Elizabeth said, "I'm so very sorry for my excitement and for knocking the sweet little bell off the wall, but most of all for the scare I gave you."

He walked to her side. "No, sweetie, I'm the one who should be sorry for being so insensitive." He folded his arms around her and she felt very secure and loved. Hot little tears trickled down her face. She reached to wipe them away as she placed her head on Scott's strong shoulder.

"Is my hair in your way, Miss Elizabeth?" His tone was sweet and so positively sincere that both of them shook with laughter.

Elizabeth went home from her meeting with Scott and decided that she would try and find out if they knew the name of the town to which Charlotte's family moved. Mama was in the kitchen, as usual, preparing supper for her husband. She cooked smaller amounts since Elizabeth had moved out, and there was only enough for the two of them.

"Wish I had known you were coming. You could have dined with us. It would have been a treat for us to have you."

"For me too, mama, but I just ran by to see if you could remember the name of the town where the Gasson's are or at least where they were."

"No, Elizabeth, I'm sorry but I don't know. I'll ask your father. Maybe he can remember. You know, we were not as close to them as you were to Charlotte. I'll see what I can find out for you. I know you would like to have her here when you and Scott get married."

"It would be so wonderful. I just can't believe how we drifted apart. Well, I need to go and do some research for a story I have in mind."

"I'm so proud of you, Elizabeth, for the way you have risen to the task of writing each week. People love your stories and your gossip column as well. Please tell me that those people that you write about are not real."

"Believe it or not, some of them are people who send in news from their community, but the parts about the arrests of the ones addicted to alcohol are fictitious."

Once in her room, Elizabeth began to try and recall the

post mark on the letters she had received from Charlotte, but she knew almost for a certainty that they had been written and mailed form the university. Elizabeth was wondering whether or not the university would supply them with any information if she and Scott made a trip there.

The only option left open to her was a census of the state of Mississippi to look up all the Matthews around twenty-three or twenty-five years of age.

"Not good, Elizabeth," she told herself. She decided that the best option she had was to hope her father could remember the name of the town to which they had moved. Things didn't seem to be too positive at the moment, but one thing Elizabeth did know was that she would keep trying. She went to sleep and dreamed the dreams of her childhood and Charlotte. "Tell it, Elizabeth!"

CHAPTER 13

*P*lans for the wedding went forward. Elizabeth wanted a white, lacy wedding gown with satin ribbons to lace the back, just as her mother had worn. She had gone to Raleigh and found one that she loved, but didn't know whether or not Scott would like it.

Corrine, Scott's sister, had made the trip with her future sister-in-law and when Elizabeth mentioned that she would like Scott's approval, Corrine came to life. "First of all, he isn't supposed to see it till you come walking down that aisle and, second of all, he won't be the one wearing the dress. This is your day. You get the dress you want, and I assure you that Scott will not complain."

"Thank you. I've been nervous as a long tailed cat in a room full of rocking chairs."

"Where in the world did you hear that expression?"

Elizabeth grinned at Corrine. "My granddad used to say it."

Elizabeth got the dress she was looking for and they returned home with thoughts of all the rest of the chores that needed to be done before the wedding. "How long do we have," Corrine asked.

"Would you believe that I don't know? We don't have a

date for the wedding!" "If you and Scott are planning a church wedding, I would suggest a visit to the church to talk with the preacher. He can tell you when the church will be available."

"Next I need to design my wedding invitation. We can print those at the office. Good for us."

Things went much better than Elizabeth could have hoped for and the day had at last arrived.

"I'll have to remember to thank Miss Paula at the bank for helping us with our finances."

Elizabeth was beyond nervous as she put the last pin into her bun.

"What if this thing falls down, Corrine?"

"It will be fine."

Elizabeth had enlisted the help of Corrine with the music for the ceremony. "Don't know why you are so nervous. It should be me. I think I must be the whole program!"

Corrine picked up her bouquet and headed for the sanctuary.

"I guess I need to warm up that old pipe organ." She left Elizabeth alone.

"This is it," she thought. "This is the big day. Oh, Charlotte, wherever you are today, I know you will be with me in spirit."

Mrs. Buie came into the little room off the narthex.

"Are you nervous, dear?"

"No, mama, but I am very excited. Do you believe that in a few minutes your little girl will be a married woman?"

Unnoticed by Elizabeth, she brushed a tear from her cheek.

"I know. I don't know that I'm ready for this, but I suppose I might as well be." Elizabeth turned and embraced her mother.

"I love you, mother, and appreciate all you have done for me. I hope you know that."

Her mother looked at her and smiled. She felt for the very first time she was seeing her daughter as she was, a beautiful young lady who was entering a new phase of her life. Elizabeth was no longer that little girl, dependent on her mother for everything. She was about to go out on an adventure which she was well equipped to handle. They heard the lovely chorus of "Oh Promise Me."

Mama kissed Elizabeth and walked out to her place in the narthex.

Elizabeth looked for her father as she walked out.

"There you are," she smiled.

"Are you ready to do this; really sure?"

"She squeezed her father's hand and said, "I don't think I have ever been more ready for anything in my entire life."

The music floated through the church and into the hall.

"Here Comes the Bride."

"Daddy, they are playing my song!"

"Well, let's get out there."

On her father's arm, Elizabeth walked to the door of the sanctuary and looked at the beautifully decorated church, but when she saw Scott Gilmore's face, she could not look away.

"Wow," she thought, "I don't think I've ever seen a more handsome man." But then she saw that there was now something different about him. Elizabeth realized that Scott cut his hair! Not too short, but noticeably shorter.

She smiled at him and thought, "I hope he didn't think he had to do that for me!" Little did she know but Scott was speechless at the very sight of her.

The preacher began asking all the preliminary questions of who would give the bride away and talked about the divine institution of holy matrimony. Finally, he reached the "I do" part and Elizabeth's heart began to race.

"Should I say I do or I will?"

Then she heard the preacher saying, "Do you, Elizabeth Torrey Buie, take Scott Thomas Gilmore to be your lawfully wedding husband?"

She decided on, "I do."

She smiled as Scott, looking lovingly into her eyes, said his "I do."

"I now pronounce you man and wife. Ladies and gentlemen, may I present to you Mr. and Mrs. Scott Thomas Gilmore."

As Elizabeth and Scott hurriedly left the church, she couldn't put into words the wonderful feeling she had, yet in the back of her mind she could hear a little voice whisper, "Tell it, Elizabeth!"

CHAPTER 14

*T*he couple took a short honeymoon trip to Raleigh. It was not ideal, but they had neither the time nor money to go anyplace farther or more expensive. They were back in the office in two days' time.

"Someone has to get the paper out." Scott knew that his father could not handle it alone.

Elizabeth was at work on her story for the week.

"Better be a good one." Scott smiled at her.

Elizabeth was eager to get under way. Sitting at her desk for the first time as the wife of the editor, she began to write.

"I believe you have met this family before. A family of four small children and their lives together in a modest home, doing things that children do. It was not a life of luxury, but love and togetherness. They played in the mud, climbed trees, had china berry wars, and just used whatever was available to occupy their time and have fun at the same time.

This particular day was different. This was the day that their number would increase from four to five. They had been ushered out of the house to the porch while inside their mother was in labor, under the watchful gaze of Mrs. Neblett, a midwife in town. The children sat on the porch in deep discussion. They were excited about the fact that there would be one more to play with.

"I hope it ain't another girl." Kenny was praying for a little brother.

"Well, we don't know what it will be till it gets here." Janice was always quick to state her opinion.

Kenny's eyes were on Catherine. "Well, Kat can tell what it is."

Christine's brow wrinkled and she looked questionably toward Catherine.

"How you do that, Kat?" she asked.

Catherine turned toward the younger ones as though she was about to impart mysterious wisdom from ancient and exotic places.

"Catherine, you know what mama said about that!"

Catherine loved to roll her eyes at any sign of what she considered ridiculous.

"I wasn't going to say anything."

Forgetting about the previous question, "Christine asked, "What are we going to call the baby"

"We have to each think up a boy name and a girl name." Janice was all about contests and games. "Then when the baby comes, we can vote on the best name." Kenny jumped to his feet. "Let's call him Buster!"

"Oh my goodness, that's the same thing you wanted to name the dog." Janice was a little upset with her little brother.

"That's his name for the baby if it's a boy," Catherine had her hands on her hips and was glaring at her sister.

"All right, Kenny votes for Buster if it's a boy," Janice said. Taking a short stub of a pencil, she wrote down her brother's choice.

"What if it's a little girl? Janice continued.

"I don't even care." Kenny was a teensy bit upset with his

sister's opinion of his boy name. In a huff, he went down the steps into the yard where he pulled a tall, slender blade of grass. Sitting beside a curious looking tiny hole in the ground, he spit on the end of the grass and extended it down into the hole. He began to chant, "Doodle bug, doodle bug."

Janice looked at him quizzically. "What in the world is he doing?"

Catherine jumped up and ran down the steps to join him. "He's fishing for doodle bugs, silly," she called over her shoulder. The name game was over as the rest of the crew ran into the yard to find their own doodle bug hole. Just then, from within the house, they heard a wee little cry. All eyes were on the back screen door as Mrs. Neblett appeared with the tiny bundle.

"It's a boy," she announced.

Kenny jumped excitedly to his feet. "It's Buster!"

Catherine rolled her eyes.

Elizabeth took her new article to Scott for his approval.

"This one is long, Elizabeth."

"I know, but I thought that since we had missed last week completely, you needed to cover more space in this week's edition."

"A wise thing to do, sweetheart."

"I'm glad you approve."

Elizabeth, I have been thinking about hiring someone to help us with articles and just things in general. Now that I have trapped you for my wife, I don't have to pay you a salary anymore and maybe we could afford to do that."

"I knew you had an ulterior motive for marrying me. You are a complete cad."

Scott picked her up and swung her around until they were both a bit dizzy.

"You know that's not true." Kissing her, he put her feet back on the floor.

"I don't know about that, but you are the one with all the business sense. I trust your decision."

"Well, thank you, madam. I appreciate that vote of confidence. We might even be able to venture out more with your stories. I was thinking maybe a sports section." Scott smiled.

"Oh, you'd really love that. The trouble is that we don't have any sports around here to write about."

"Elizabeth, everyone loves baseball and only six or seven years ago they played the first major league game. It was Cleveland Forest City and Ft. Wayne. It's just going to keep growing. I'll bet that one day in the future, you ladies will have a team or two of your own."

"Now you are being ridiculous, Scott, but if that ever happens, I'll be the one to cover it."

"Along those lines, I have been in touch with some guys I know who are reporters for newspapers in other areas and they cover sports."

"I'll bet you already have someone in mind to help us out at the paper, don't you?"

"Are we about to have our first squabble, Elizabeth?"

"What's his name, Scott, and what does he expect to get paid?"

"My goodness! It's still just an idea rattling around in my head."

"Does that rattle have a name, Scott?"

"Well, I do have some ideas."

"What's your best one, Mr. Editor?"

"There is this one guy who knows all about baseball. He is a walking rule book and truly loves the game. He hopes to become a coach someday. I haven't even said anything to him about a job because we more than likely couldn't even afford him." Scott waited for a response and hearing none, he continued. "His name is Brian, Brian Wilks."

"Ok, let's find out if he is willing to think about it and then we can fuss about it." Scott contacted Brian by sending a telegraph to him to explain the situation at the paper and make him an offer. The next morning at the newspaper office the telegram and the reply from Brian came. It read: "Would like to help you out. Stop. I am flattered. Stop. Couldn't even eat on salary. Stop. Let me know when salary changes. Stop."

As Scott read the reply, he smiled and thought, "Why am I surprised? I wouldn't have gone for that either." He handed the telegram to Elizabeth.

"I don't even have to look at the reply. I know what the answer is. Who would want to take on all the pressure that a newspaper puts on an individual for such a small salary?"

"Why didn't you kick me before I sent the telegram?"

"If I had stopped you, you would always be wondering whether or not he would have accepted."

"I guess you are right. We aren't really able to take on anyone else just now and still eat."

"It seems that he might consider the position if the salary is right. We won't give up just yet. We will just have to tighten up and keep doing the work ourselves." "How did I ever survive without you?"

"That's one that I'm still working on, Scott."

He walked over to her desk and sat down in her chair. Taking her by the hand, he sat her down in his lap. "Have I told you today how very much I adore you?" "I think I remember something like that, but just for good measure, tell me again."

"I love you, Elizabeth Buie Gilmore."

CHAPTER 15

ork continued at the newspaper with only two to labor. Elizabeth decided on another story this week because of all the work that had to be done and the space that had to be filled. Not much had been happening in the communities and all the news that had been sent to them was not enough to fill her column. Once again Elizabeth put on the persona of Hilda W. Roy and began to tell her story. This one had come from her grandfather and would take only a few embellishments to complete. She wrote:

"The children were in the yard. The sun had set and the moon had begun her journey across the sky. Gleeful squeals of the children could be heard as they ran to and fro through the yard with cleanly washed mason jars. The dark of the night made it easy to follow the objects of their joy. The lightning bugs were out in great numbers and as the children caught them, they would place them in the jar, tighten the cap and move on to the next. It was always a contest to see who could catch the most bugs and light up the largest area.

"I've got the most!" Christine would shout.

"No! I have sixteen hundred." Kenny was looking at his jar as though he was counting.

The sound of bullfrogs could be heard coming from the ditch.

"Shhh," Janice called for silence. "Let all the lightning bugs go 'cause we are going to get bull frogs."

Catherine was reluctant at first because she remembered what her mother had said about snakes.

"I don't know, we could catch something we don't want," Catherine frowned a little.

"Like what?" Christine asked with eyes wide and head slightly tilted.

"Like a big, nasty old water moccasin," she said in hushed tones.

Christine let out a shrill shriek and ran for the comfort and safety of the house.

"Scaredy cat." Kenny wasn't about to be the next one to retreat.

The three moved cautiously to the ditch.

"Yeowww!" Janice screamed, but not loudly enough for mama to hear.

Looking at Janice, Catherine demanded, "What is wrong with you?"

"I thought a snake was on my foot, but it was just a stick I stepped on. A big stick!"

Catherine rolled her eyes. "Janice, did you bring a sack?"

"As a matter of fact, I grabbed one from the porch when I heard the croaking. Look for the eyes."

Grabbing everything that was above the water in the ditch, the children caught bullfrogs – big bullfrogs. They were diligent with the frog grabbing until mama's voice was heard calling them to come inside.

"Christine has told mama we are in the ditch. I just know she has."

Janice tied up the end of the old pillow case and the three

headed back to the porch. Mama watched as they opened the bag with their catch. Frogs began to hop, and Kenny chased them. When all the slimy, green amphibians were counted and returned to the bag, they had counted seventeen.

"My stars!" mama said, "This will make a very nice supper tomorrow night." Janice looked at Catherine as the fate of the frogs became apparent.

"You mean you want to kill them and fry 'em up?"

"Why, of course, they are delicious with some good old biscuits and maybe some fresh corn and tomatoes from the garden."

Kenny was rubbing his hands together and muttering something closely akin to "Yummmm."

"We will put them in this big old pail with water on them and they will last till morning very well."

They knew that it was time for bed and after bathing, they put on night clothes and got into bed. Janice and Christine slept together in the same bed, but Catherine didn't like for anyone to touch her, so she got the smaller bed. Christine soon feel asleep and Janice crept over to Catherine's bed.

"Hey, get in your own bed," was the greeting she received.

"I'm just thinking about the poor old bull frogs we caught. Tomorrow they will die."

"So what do you want to do?" Catherine was interested in saving the condemned frogs.

Janice leaned in to whisper her plan for the release of the bull frogs.

"No one would ever know if the two of us slipped outside and turned over that bucket so they could escape back to their ditch."

"We would get the fire beat out of us if daddy found out we had let a dinner just hop back to the ditch!"

Janice pleaded, "He wouldn't ever need to find out. Christine and Kenny are asleep and won't even know. I bet Christine would help if she were awake, and Kenny would if he didn't want to eat them so much."

"Okay, I'll do it for the frogs, not just because you want to do this, but if you ever tell, I'll hunt you down."

"I don't want a whupping any more than you do. Let's go."

The two made their way on tip toe to the back door. The screen door creaked as they opened it, and Janice wet in her pants just a little at the thought of being discovered. They closed the door very quietly and walked down the steps to the back yard with the pail of frogs. The night was dark as pitch except for the lightning bugs that flitted around over the yard.

"It's way too dark to go all the way to the ditch to let these frogs go." Janice was getting a little more concerned. Concerned about getting caught releasing frogs, but also about the snakes that may be out and about. She had heard that snakes ate frogs and she didn't want to be present when the dinner bell rang.

In one swoop, Janice lifted the top on the pail and dropped her side of the load. To add insult to injury, she ran and left Catherine holding the evidence of the great frog escape.

"Wait, you coward. This was your idea."

"Get the bucket and make sure all the frogs are out. I'll wait on the porch for you."

"I don't know why I ever listen to you."

Shaking the last two frogs out of the pail, Catherine made her way to the porch with blood in her eyes.

The next morning, the children were up with the smell of eggs cooking.

Janice whispered to Catherine, "At least we know what we are not having. Frogs for breakfast!" She smiled at her joke and looked at Catherine.

Catherine rolled her eyes.

Elizabeth approached Scott, story in hand. "Here you go, my love, a nice long story for you."

"Great, what's it about?"

"Well, it's about frogs if you must know."

"Frogs? Are you teasing me? Frogs?"

"Just read the story, Scott. If you don't like it, you can write another one, or pay Brian a decent salary so he can help you."

"Man, is that an attitude you're throwing at me?"

"Maybe or maybe it's just to get your attention. You can decide for yourself."

Elizabeth walked out the front door and left Scott with his mouth agape.

As Scott was scratching his head in awe, the door opened and a smiling Elizabeth stuck her head back inside. "I love the editor of this newspaper, but I find that I have to keep him on his toes. Don't be late for dinner. We're having frog legs."

CHAPTER 16

*I*t was the weekend and Elizabeth had decided to check on her mother. She had been nursing a severe sinus infection and Elizabeth wanted to take her some soup and visit with her for a while. As she always did, she decided because it was only a short distance from their apartment that she would walk. It was a beautiful day in late June, not too hot, and Elizabeth was enjoying her leisurely stroll. Her old street was none the worse for the time it had been there and all the past history it had endured.

She could see her old friend, Charlotte's, house up ahead. "Looks like someone has taken care of it," she observed. Upon closer examination, she noticed a stiff, card board sign beside the walk way. It read, "For Sale." She hurried on down the street and walking inside her childhood home, called to her mother.

"I'm in the parlor, dear."

Elizabeth greeted her mother with a kiss on the cheek and setting the warm soup on the table, took a seat beside her.

"Mother, did you know that Charlotte's old house is up for sale?"

"Why, no, Elizabeth, I didn't know that, but I don't suppose anyone has occupied it since the Gassons moved."

"I really need to find out who owns that house now. Maybe it can lead me to Charlotte."

"I'll ask your father to see what he can find out."

"Thank you, mama. Now, what seems to be your main ailment?"

"Oh, I just have a nagging little cold. Nothing to be too concerned about. It just makes me feel tired all the time."

"Mama, I want you to promise me that you will start taking better care of yourself."

Her mother smiled and asked Elizabeth to find her a spoon from the kitchen so that she might try the warm soup Elizabeth had made for her.

Elizabeth was not an accomplished cook, but she had been taught how to make chicken soup by her mother, and it was the best item in her box of recipes. She hurried back with a spoon for her mother and waited anxiously for mama to taste her offering.

"Why, Elizabeth, it's delicious. Much better than mine!"

Elizabeth was pleased but knew what her mother would say even before she tasted it.

"If that were only true, mama, I would serve it to Scott every day."

"Elizabeth, you are your own worse critic."

"That's what Scott tells me."

"How is Scott?"

"Oh, he's fine, mama. He is looking forward to coming over this Christmas. He says that he wants to taste those Jesus cookies. You are planning on making them this year, I hope."

"Well, I had planned on doing just that, in case I had some company. They would be much better if we had little ones to share the story with."

"Now, mama, Scott and I plan on having children, only not till we make the business a little more profitable."

"Well, don't wait too long. I miss hearing little squeals and having little feet running through the house."

"Mama, you know I never ran through the house; daddy wouldn't allow that." "You were always chattering though, and we knew you were a happy little girl. I sometimes regret that you didn't have a sibling to keep you company."

The two visited until early evening and Elizabeth jumped to her feet. "I had no idea that I had stayed for so long. I really need to get home and warm up the rest of the soup for Scott. I'm anxious to get his opinion about my best dish."

Elizabeth kissed her mother, saying that she would check on her the next day. Out the door she went and back down the street toward her own apartment. As she walked upon the Gasson's old house, she slowed her pace slightly, and remembering her childhood days once again, was drawn back to the backyard by some unexplainable force. The China berry tree was still there with the small green balls just waiting for someone to start a war.

Elizabeth picked four off the stem and proceeded to throw them in the direction the garden had been.

"Everything is here except Charlotte." She walked over to the big oak and sat down on the cool, green moss. She leaned her head back against the tree. A flood of memories were released and she felt a salty tear trickle down her cheek. As she ran her hand over the velvety moss, she could feel the joy that she had so many years ago playing with silk haired corn babies and the imaginary princess dresses that they wore. Elizabeth did not know exactly how long she sat under the tree, but before she knew it, the sun was setting and she knew that Scott would be worried. She jumped up from her magic moss and brushed her skirt off.

"I simply have to find Charlotte. Maybe daddy can get me some information when he enquires about the house." Her thoughts returned to the present and her husband. She bounded up the steps and into the apartment.

"Where have you been? I've been worried about you."

"I went to check on mama and take her some soup. She's been feeling poorly." "She okay?"

"It's a sinus infection, but she'll be fine. I took her some of your supper."

"I saw some cold soup on the stove, but I don't care for cold soup."

"Well, my dear, did you ever think of warming it up?"

"To be honest, no, I don't know how."

"Poor little thing."

Elizabeth's lips were pouty with insincere sympathy. She heated up the soup for Scott and then began to tell him about the Gasson house being up for sale. "That's a good lead to pursue." Scott was all involved with his chicken soup.

"Elizabeth, this is really good."

"I'm glad you like it, but I want to discuss something else with you. We are doing fairly well with the business, and I was wondering what you thought about checking into the possibility of purchasing the Gasson house. You know this apartment is way too small for us. We need more room, and we could talk with Miss Paula at the bank about financing."

"How long have you been thinking about this, sweetheart?"

"Just today, but it is a good idea."

"Do you think that maybe you went by Charlotte's old house and just got a little bit nostalgic?"

"Maybe a little, but we could do it. We both have savings accounts and that ought to cover a down payment. Just think Scott, our very own home. Doesn't that sound great?"

"It's a big step, Elizabeth. I think we should think about it and get a little more information."

"I have mama working on that. I asked her to see if daddy could find out some of the particulars."

Scott promised to give her idea some thought and sat down to finish his soup, which had become cold again.

"That was great, sweetheart, but I have to run back to the office to finish up some last minute things."

"Do you need me to help?"

"No, dear, nothing you can do. I already have your article."

Elizabeth was very happy that Scott didn't need her. She had not been feeling quite herself for a couple of days, and it seemed to be getting a little worse.

"I must have picked up a bug. I hope I didn't add to mama's discomfort by passing something else on to her."

Feeling slightly dizzy, Elizabeth headed for the comfort of her bed to lie down.

She did not intend to tell Scott because she thought it would give him something extra to worry about. The next morning she felt better and got dressed for church. After Scott's famous pancake breakfast, Elizabeth felt her dizziness begin to return.

"Scott, you go to church without me today. I feel a little bit dizzy."

"You okay?"

"I'll be fine, Scott. I'm just a little tired. I didn't sleep well last night."

"I'll just stay at home with you in case you need me."

"I'd rather you go to church. I just want to put my feet up and rest for a while."

"I can tell when I'm not wanted." Scott looked for a smile, which he received from Elizabeth.

The next day Elizabeth did not feel much better, waking up with a slightly nauseous feeling. Scott insisted she stay at home and rest one more day. Elizabeth was happy to oblige and felt that a trip to visit the doctor might be in order, just to ward off any further complications. After Scott left for the office, Elizabeth got dressed and rode to the doctor's office with a friend who lived in the apartment next to hers. She was an office keeper for Dr. Jobe, her own doctor. "I'm glad you are riding with me this morning. This little buggy is a bit bumpy, but it's better than walking." Her friend was very nice and trying to get some kind of experience in nursing.

Elizabeth was the first patient in the office and was happy to think she would be out quickly. Her father's office was only two buildings down from Dr. Jobe's office. He would give her a ride home if she didn't feel like walking. The office was neat and clean, but smelled like a doctor's office, sterile.

"Come in, Miss Elizabeth." Dr. Jobe's smiling face had appeared from behind his examination room door. He held the door for Elizabeth and asked, "What seems to be bothering you today? Never knew you to have anything worse than a sore throat and the sniffles. Sit up here on the table and let's have a look at you."

"I've been a little dizzy for the past two days and this morning I felt a bit sick to my stomach."

"How long have you been married, Elizabeth?" Dr. Jobe smiled as he listened to Elizabeth's heart.

"About a year or so, Dr. Jobe."

"You like this man a lot, do you?"

"Oh, he's wonderful."

Dr. Jobe continued his examination asking more questions until he felt he had the correct diagnosis. Pulling his glasses down on his nose, he smiled at Elizabeth.

"I would say that you might think about enlarging your house. I think you and your young man are going to be parents."

"Are you sure?"

"Well, reasonably sure, but you will know soon enough. You are late, nauseous, and the smell of bacon cooking makes you sick."

"I can't believe it!"

"Well, it happens sometimes to people who are married." Dr. Job laughed at Elizabeth's excitement.

"Please don't tell Scott or my mama. I want to wait till I'm one hundred percent sure."

"I would never be so insensitive. That's half the fun, being able to spring the news on the husband."

"When would you say it will be born?"

"If you have given me all the right information, I'd say early April, around Easter."

Thanking the doctor and forgetting to pay for her visit, she hurried down the street to her father's office. Trying to control her excitement, she went inside to find her father reading the morning paper. He lowered the paper upon hearing someone come inside. Seeing Elizabeth, he smiled.

"Well, to what do I owe this honor? Anything wrong?"

Elizabeth smiled and kissed her father on the cheek.

"Nothing wrong. I just decided to drop in to see you on my walk. I'm kind of tired, too. Thought I'd try and talk you into a ride back home."

"I would just be delighted."

Elizabeth was fairly bursting to blurt out her news to her father, but wanted to be completely sure before she did. They rode in the bright black buggy home, the wheels making a happy, clicking sound as they turned.

"Have you seen one of those horseless carriages, papa? You ought to get one for you and mama to drive around in town."

"Horses are more dependable and they go where you want them to go, most of the time. Can you just imagine sharing this tiny street with a machine?"

They both laughed and father pulled the reign to stop the horse in front of Elizabeth's apartment. Kissing her father on the cheek, she thanked him and walked inside.

"I don't know how long I can keep this information to myself," she thought. "A baby!" She rubbed her stomach. "I sure hope it's a girl … yes, indeed, no doubt what her name will be."

CHAPTER 17

Elizabeth was feeling much better the next day upon finding out about her condition. She and Scott went to the office together that day.

"You sure you are up to this, sweetheart?" Scott cast a cautious glance at his wife.

"I feel wonderful," she smiled at Scott. "I can't tell you how good I feel."

"Well, you certainly had a miraculous recovery and now, get in there and write me a story."

She smiled lovingly at Scott and sat down at her desk.

"I think maybe I'll tell my story of Charlotte this week since she has been so much on my mind. She began:

"Have you ever had a best friend? This one special friend with whom you share all your secrets and dreams? I had that friend. She stays with me every day, although I have not seen nor talked with her in years. She moved away and we lost touch. I miss her every day and hope against hope that I will find her again, and we will sit and talk the way we did when we were children. I told Charlotte one day the story of the Jesus cookies we make at home on East Sunday and I will share it now with you.

Mama made the Jesus cookies only twice a year and all the children in the neighborhood would look forward to the day when they could come to my house and eat Jesus cookies. The cookies are delicious, but even better than the cookies is the story behind them and what it means in the life of a Christian.

It's a story that needs to be told often and no only on Easter Sunday... This is the story of the Jesus cookies.

'Jesus cookies tell the story of the death and resurrection of our Lord Jesus Christ. Jesus was arrested and beaten by Roman soldiers in the same way that we break up the pecans for the cookies by pounding them with the wooden spoon to break them into pieces. While dying on the cross, Jesus asked for water and the soldiers gave him vinegar, so we add one teaspoon of vinegar into a large mixing bowl. Next, separate the eggs and add the whites to the vinegar. The eggs represent life and Jesus gave His life so that we might have eternal life. We sprinkle a dash of salt in to represent the tears shed by those saddened at the death of Jesus. At this point, things in the bowl would not taste very good, but next comes the sugar. Jesus died because He loves us and that's the sweetest part of the story. The eggs are beaten until we see a pearly white color in the bowl. White is a symbol for the purity God sees in those who have been cleansed from sin by Jesus' death. The nuts are folded into the mixture and dropped from a teaspoon onto a cookie sheet. Each cookie mound represents a rocky tomb like the one in which Jesus' body was placed. The cookies are placed inside a heated oven, the door closed and the oven turned off. Jesus' tomb was sealed, so we place a long piece of tape across the oven door. Then, it's off to bed. Children may feel sad and disappointed to leave the cookies, just as Jesus' disciples felt sad to leave him in the sealed tomb. On Easter morning, the oven door is opened to expose gleaming white cookies. When a bite is taken from a cookie, we find that they are empty or hollow inside. Jesus' followers found His tomb open and empty. He had risen!' This story of the Jesus cookies is told to others to show the sacrifice Jesus made to save us. If you believe Jesus died for you so long ago, I would leave you with two words about this story. Tell it!

When I shared this story with my friend, Charlotte, on that day, the look on her face was surprising. It was somewhere between sad and confused. I couldn't decide what I had said in my story to cause the reaction that I got. She asked me if the Jews thought Jesus was the Messiah, and I told her that I didn't think so, but the disciples and followers of Jesus sure did. Charlotte stood up slowly and told me that she and her parents were Jews. It was as though she thought that I was accusing the whole Jewish race for crucifying Jesus. She was deeply hurt and walked out of my house without a word. I had hurt my friend deeply and did not realize what I had done. I think of Charlotte every day and pray that one day I will find her and tell her how sorry I am for hurting her in that way. I believe she will understand when I tell her how important it is for Christians to share their faith by telling others about Jesus, who gave His life for us. I had to realize that it is not for me to pick and choose to whom I tell the Good News, but it is my job to tell it."

"Here's my story, Scott, I hope you will use it."

"Now why wouldn't I use your story? I always love the things you write."

"I just told the story about the Jesus cookies and what they mean. People feel differently about this story. You never know how it will affect them, but I guess that is best left to God."

"Absolutely right, sweetheart. Thank you for this article. I may run it twice. Once now and once at Easter time. Go home and rest. I love you."

Elizabeth thought to herself what a good father that her

Scott was going to be. She really wanted to turn around and run into Scott's arms and shout, "You're going to be a daddy at Easter time!" But Elizabeth settled for going home to a big bowl of fresh peaches she had been craving all day. She was ready for the walk home, which was actually not that far. "After all, she thought, I need to be getting more exercise. It's good for the baby."

As she walked by the boarding house in which she once lived, Miss Claireece was out sweeping the walk way in front of her building.

"Well, Elizabeth, what pep you have in your step this day. Child, your face is so happy looking that it makes me not feel so bad about having to sweep this walk. Have you been running? Your face looks flushed."

Elizabeth thought she had better hurry on because Miss Claireece was so good at figuring things out. She was very much afraid she would discover that Elizabeth was pregnant.

"No, Miss Claireece, I wasn't running, just in a hurry to get home to some fresh peaches I have been thinking about all morning."

As she hurried down the street, she hoped Miss Claireece would not think of her craving peaches and figure out her secret.

"This is going to be hard to do so maybe I ought to go ahead and spill the beans. How dumb. No, I won't spill the beans, but I have never been able to keep a secret very well. I remember when I told Charlotte's middle name to mama and that was supposed to be a secret." She had reached her apartment and thought, "Thank goodness, I haven't told anybody yet except that old tom cat back there in the alley, and he didn't even seem to care."

Elizabeth made a bee line for the fresh peaches in the bowl on the kitchen table, and picking out a nice sharp knife, began to peel and cut up two and put them in a bowl. "A little cream would be nice on these and just a sprinkling of sugar. Gracious! If I start all this eating, I will be as big as a cow." She sat down on the sofa and cradled the bowl close to her chest as though someone may try to steal her treasure. She finished her peaches and cream in short order and considered having another bowl. Deciding against the idea because of the extra pounds, she turned to the book shelf to find some reading material. She picked out a book call, "The Adventures of Tom Sawyer" by Mark Twain. She opened the book, settled back to read and fell sound asleep. She woke to the sound of the door opening and a voice calling, "Elizabeth, are you here?"

"Elizabeth, your mother sent a boy to tell me that your father is not well. He has experienced some chest pain and she called the doctor to come over and check on him. I thought we might need to go over there and check on him also."

Elizabeth's heart leaped and she jumped to her feet. "Oh, Scott, he can't be sick, not now."

They climbed into the buggy for the short ride to the Buie's house.

"Settle down, Elizabeth. He is going to be fine." Scott tried to be reassuring.

Elizabeth ran ahead of Scott into the house. Dr. Jobe was coming out of her father's room. Elizabeth caught his arm. "Is daddy all right, doctor?" Her voice was tense with concern.

"He is fine, Elizabeth. He just had a strong case of indigestion and gas."

Elizabeth breathed a sigh of relief and thanked Dr. Jobe.

"He just needs to stay in bed for that anti-acid medication to do its job and he will be fit as a fiddle."

Elizabeth walked into his room. "What in the world have you been eating to give you such a case of indigestion? I was worried sick."

Her father smiled. "It had to be those fresh peaches I ate this morning. I got some from John Martin's farm this past week, and I guess maybe I just made a pig of myself."

Elizabeth plopped down on the edge of her father's bed.

"You trying to bounce me out of the bed, Elizabeth?"

"I'm sorry, daddy, I didn't mean to sit down so hard, but I was just thinking that I ate a big bowl of Mr. Martin's peaches today also."

"Well, they must have put some bound in both of us. You nearly bounced me right out of the bed when you sat down."

They both laughed, but Elizabeth wondered what she would have done if something had happened to her father before she had a chance to tell him that he was going to be a grandfather at Easter time. Life was so uncertain. It made Elizabeth rethink her decision to wait to tell her news. But if there was no baby, it would be disappointing. She decided she would wait a few days longer. She decided to spend her time wisely and write another short story for Scott. She wrote:

"This is a story about friends. I know, we all have them, but do you have one that stands out in your memory, one that is extra special? I'm talking about sister close, do anything for you close, be there no matter where you are close. This story is about such a friendship. These friends even shared the same name. These Sarah's had eight children between them. They lived in the same town, and when they were young, their children thought they were brothers and sisters, just lived in different houses. They played outside, as all children do, and only came inside when they were called. Most of the things they did were done together. There was one whole week when it rained every day and most areas had been inundated with large amounts of water, especially around the numerous small lakes and ponds in the delta. This meant an abundant supply of the one thing already naturally found in this area – crawfish!

It seemed a good idea by both the Sarah's to go crawfishing and have a big crawfish boil. With all the children to hunt, there was the assurance of a big haul. The two gathered up the children and piled into an old wagon for the trip to the pond just beyond the Roark house. All the children were excited and bragging about who would catch the most crawfish. They soon arrived at the pond, although the mule had a hard time pulling such a load in the soft mud. At the pond, the children jumped from the wagon and set about the task of crawfishing. Each one was barefooted and had been reminded by the Sarah's to watch out for snakes and not to poke their fingers into any holes. The two Sarah's sat in the front of the wagon and began to survey the scene that was already filled with a small army of children running and screaming; and yes, sticking their fingers down small holes in search of the illusive crawfish. The two Sarah's observed strange mini mounds of mud that protruded above the land. These mounds were made of tiny balls of mud that surrounded holes in the ground. Obviously, homes that the crawfish had erected for themselves.

"Well," said one of the Sarah's, "go do some crawfishing."

"Just how would you have me do that, Miss Sarah?"

"See those holes and mounds of dirt?"

"Yes, I do."

"Well, go out there and stick your finger in that hole and call the crawfish."

"You think I'm crazy? You go and do it."

"Okay, I'm right behind you."

Debbie got stuck in the mud and Kris was right there to pull her out. Kris had made Debbie her own charge.

The hunt went on for about an hour, with children falling down in the mud, getting pinched by the prey and laughing until the Sarah's called time. They said that some had wet their pants, but no one could say for sure because of all the mud.

Each child had put their crawfish into a galvanized pail they brought from home.

"How many we got?" Linda asked, eyes shining with anticipation.

One Sarah looked into the pail and the other one smiled. "I count 12. Twelve big craw dads!"

"Oh, man, that's not even enough to eat." Debbie was disappointed.

One Sarah looked at the other Sarah and asked, "How many of us are there?"

"Let's see, I count 12. Wow, Miss Debbie that means we get one crawfish each! Yum!"

Kris picked Debbie up lovingly and sat her in the wagon. Crawling in beside her, she put her arms around little Debbie and hugged her.

"Don't you worry, my baby, I'm giving you my crawfish."

Did you ever have friends like these? If you did, you have been blessed with a special gift from God. If you haven't, you need to just keep on looking.

CHAPTER 18

By the second week of August, Elizabeth was certain that she was, indeed, a lady-in-waiting. The one thing to decide now would be how she would tell Scott. It would have to be unique. At one time she thought she would tell him in her next article, but that would take too long. The next day, Elizabeth told Scott that she had some errands to run and would be taking off the afternoon.

"Sure, sweetheart, I think I've got it under control."

Elizabeth left and went to the apartment after purchasing pink and blue crepe paper streamers. She strung the paper everywhere she could reach. When she was satisfied with the look, she went into the kitchen to begin baking a cake for the occasion; dinner would be simple. First of all, because of her culinary skills, or lack thereof, and because she simply lacked the time it took to make a lavish meal, she decided to make her famous chicken soup and have a nice salad with toasted bread.

"That's awful," she thought. "Scott is probably so sick of soup." She went on with her plan and began to boil the chicken for the soup. Elizabeth had left Scott wondering what errands she so suddenly had to run.

"Maybe I'll just go home a little early and see what she

is up to." He quickly put the paper to bed and locked up the little office. All the way home, he wondered if he had forgotten some important event. Arriving home as quietly as he could, he fairly sneaked in at the front door. Opening the door, Scott was immediately met with crepe paper floating down into his face.

"Woah!" he shouted.

Alarmed at Scott's presence, she burst into the parlor where he was rubbing his hand across his face frantically. Seeing Elizabeth, Scott looked confused.

"I thought a spider was on my face. What is all this? Did I forget a birthday or an anniversary? Maybe National wave paper in your house day."

"Scott, you have spoiled the surprise."

"No, I'd say that I really am surprised. I just don't know the reason."

"Well, that makes sense."

"No, Elizabeth, it doesn't make sense. You need to explain it to me."

Elizabeth smiled her little smile. "Sit down, Scott, and I will see if I can explain it to you."

"I really wish you would."

Scott was still a little wounded by the fact that Elizabeth had pulled this little surprise on him.

"Sit down, Scott."

"Why must I sit down, Elizabeth? Has someone died and we are celebrating?"

"Now, Scott, you just need to calm down. Come over and sit on the sofa beside me."

Scott sat down. "Okay, let's have it."

"Why do you think I decorated with all these pink and blue streamers, Scott?"

"That's what I have been trying to figure out."

She took his hands and patted them gently. She looked

lovingly into his eyes and very calmly said, "Pink is for girls and blue is for boys."

"What?" Suddenly, the confused look left his face. He had figured it out. A ridiculous grin covered his face. He grabbed Elizabeth in a bear hug and immediately, thinking of her delicate condition, released the squeeze.

"Are you sure, sweetheart? When will be baby be born?"

"In April, around Easter time."

"We have to tell everybody. Have you told your parents yet?"

"Scott, you know that I wouldn't tell anyone before you knew, besides I want both of us to tell our parents."

"Elizabeth, I just love you so much! I really have to get busy with this house business. We will need more room for sure."

The next day Scott was busy making plans.

"I need to hire someone to help me at the paper so Elizabeth won't have to come in any more. I want her to take it easy."

The next thing to consider was the house. He called Miss Paula and set up an appointment to speak with her.

"Must be nice to have such a posh job as a bank officer, especially when you are a lady. Not many of those, but it does help when your daddy owns the bank." Scott decided to check with Dennis Brown, a young man that he had considered previously to help at the paper. He would see Dennis at the town meeting tonight and could talk with him then. Scott was feeling pretty good about how he was handling this situation. He sat down to think of any other problems this new event would bring.

"Problems?" He was a little ashamed of the way he thought of this birth. He found that he was so completely happy with the thought of himself being a father that nothing else occupied his mind.

Elizabeth and Scott decided to invite their parents over to their apartment to tell them the good news. Since Elizabeth had completely forgotten about the cake she had baked for the unveiling of the birth to Scott, she decided to have it when the parents came over.

"What do you think we should say, Scott?"

"Why not just that we are having a baby?"

"Oh, you had better just let me tell them."

Scott smiled and nodded his head in agreement.

A soft knock on the door announced the arrival of one set of parents. Scott ushered his parents into the parlor. Elizabeth brought the coffee server in and sat it on a table in front of the couch. Another knock.

"That will be the Buie's."

Scott went to the door to greet the guests. Mrs. Buie came in first. "What a treat," she said sitting in a big over-stuffed chair near the fireplace.

"We have been wondering what occasion this could be. Maybe an anniversary or maybe that you have come across a house that you like and decided to buy. I know Elizabeth asked her father about the Gasson's old place. Don't keep us in suspense."

Elizabeth slid forward slightly in her chair. "In a way it does have something to do with the house and our needing more room. We need more room for lots of reasons, but I think you will like the main reason for our concern best. Scott and I are expecting your first grandchild the first part of April."

Initially, there was silence and then the men rose quickly from their chairs and Scott's dad was patting him on the back and congratulating him. Mr. Buie went first to his daughter and kissed her on the cheek. There were some tears from the ladies, who chattered wildly about the time of arrival and what each one would do for Elizabeth at that time. They all moved into a semi-circle around Elizabeth, smiling and asking questions about baby clothes and the specific time of arrival.

Would it be hot? Everyone ventured a guess. Finally, Elizabeth stood up and interrupted, "Would anyone like some cake and coffee? If someone doesn't eat this cake soon, I will be forced to throw it away."

Scott walked over to his wife and put his arms around her. He couldn't help but smile as he watched everyone reacting to the news that they had just heard.

CHAPTER 19

Elizabeth's pregnancy was going very well. Occasionally, she felt that Scott was too cautious and over protective, but she knew he was just trying to keep any harm from coming to her and the baby. He had hired an older man who had at one time been a sports writer, but now retired. James Miller loved the business and had heard that Scott needed help through Mr. Gilmore, Scott's father. James had proven to be quite an asset and Elizabeth still contributed her articles to the paper.

"Do you miss your sports reporting, James?" Scott had been wanting to get to know James a little better, so he took the few minutes he had for lunch to sit and chat with him while they enjoyed a little dessert with their coffee. It would be a good start for the afternoon.

"You know, Scott, sometimes I do wish for the old days and meeting ball players. It was a lot of fun, but I didn't like the deadlines we had to make. Sometimes those were brutal."

"I guess you met lots of big league players."

"I did, Scott, but the part I enjoyed most was watching rookies get into the big league and become successful."

"I'm sure it was sad to see the once hopeful not realize their dream."

"Yes, I remember one young lad in particular from Mississippi. He was a pretty fair ball player too. Had a good bat and, man, could he play second base!"

"He didn't make it?"

"No, he messed his elbow up and that was the end of a promising career. Had a pretty little wife who gave him all the support she could."

"That's a shame."

"Yes, old Matthew could really have gone places if he hadn't messed up that knee."

"Well, I guess we had better go places too. We need to get that type set for Elizabeth's article she gave me."

Scott was excited about having a sports writer on staff although he didn't anticipate using him for that, he didn't make enough money to do that kind of reporting. His main job was just to pick up where Elizabeth left off, with things that normally needed to be done around the office. James simply loved to be in close proximity of the smell of ink and sound of the printing press. In his spare time, James loved to pick up old copies of the paper and read parts of them. He especially enjoyed reading Elizabeth's stories and articles about the locals and the community news section.

Scott had talked with Miss Paula and the seller of the old Gasson place. They had come to an amicable agreement on price and the papers had all been signed. Today was the first day that Scott and Elizabeth would have access to the house and Scott was very anxious to get home.

"Hey," James called as he was about to leave for the day, "if you need any help with the move, my son and I are really good at it. We have moved so much, I think I could have a moving business."

Scott thanked him and added, "If you are really serious, I'll talk with you tomorrow."

"The wife is out of town so if there's anything in the way of moving to be done tonight, I can come by and help."

"Man, that's great. I have some heavy boxes that Elizabeth can't help me with. I'd really be afraid for her to even try."

"I could finally meet this super woman with all the talent."

"Come on by about seven. I'd ask you to come to supper, but I don't have any idea what Elizabeth is cooking. If it's not chicken soup or Jesus cookies, we might be in for trouble."

Scott got home and kissed Elizabeth. Giving her tummy a little rub, he headed for the kitchen. On the table was a delicious looking dinner of country fried steak, mashed potatoes and little green peas.

"Wow," Scott was smiling down at the meal.

"Did your mother come by today and cook?"

Elizabeth's countenance changed immediately. Noticing the change and realizing that he had been too harsh with his teasing, he went to his wife.

"Sweetheart, I'm sorry. I was just teasing. I'm sure that you had to work hard to achieve this beautiful meal you cooked for me."

"No, I didn't. Mama did come over and she did most of the cooking."

They both laughed and Scott sat down to his lovely dinner.

"James is coming by tonight to help me move those heavy boxes into the house. He's such a nice person. We had a nice conversation today at lunch, and I got to know him a little bit better. I think he's going to work out nicely for us at the paper. I may even get him to write about some of his experiences as a sports writer. I think people would enjoy hearing about how some of their baseball heroes got into the big league."

"He seems very nice. I'm really glad that he offered to give you some help with the box moving. I don't think your father would have been up for that."

There was a knock at the door.

"That must be old James. He told me his wife was out of town. Guess he doesn't have anything to do, so he came early."

"Shall we invite him to eat dinner?"

"Eat what, Elizabeth? I have eaten it all."

Elizabeth laughed as Scott went to the door to welcome James.

"Did I make it on time?" James smiled and followed Scott into the parlor. "I hope you told your wife that you invited me to dinner."

Elizabeth looked a little embarrassed and Scott was quick to tell her that James was only teasing. He was also quite hopeful that James would not mention his comment about her cooking skills.

Always the good hostess, Elizabeth offered them coffee and pie before they began their laborious task. James graciously declined, but Scott, who was not used to being served dessert, said that he might need the sugar for energy.

Elizabeth went into the kitchen and brought back a dainty little saucer with a thick slice of pecan pie placed in the center of the dish and a discreet mound of Whipped cream gracing the top.

James eyed the tempting treat. At length, Elizabeth smiled at James,

"Are you sure you won't just try a small piece of my pie? I think you might like it."

"Well, maybe just a small sliver, but not too small."

"Elizabeth's mother made the pie." Scott wanted to get it right this time.

The look on Elizabeth's face told Scott at once that either he had said too much again, or Elizabeth had in fact made the pie herself.

In an attempt to redeem himself, Scott said, "Sweetheart, did you make this wonderful pie?"

"Why, yes, Scott, I actually did make that pie. Do you truly think that all your wife can make is chicken soup?"

James put his fork down on the side of his saucer. "May I say, Elizabeth, this has got to be the best pecan pie I have ever eaten. I can tell that you are quite a cook in your own right."

Scott had dodged the bullet once again and breathed a sigh of relief. The two men brought the boxes to the door, and since the Gasson's old house was just down the street, Scott pulled out a little wagon that had been his in childhood and began to load the boxes onto its bed. As the two made their way down the walkway toward the old Gasson place, Scott made an observation.

"You sure have a talent for getting a guy into trouble."

"Women are just over sensitive when they are in the family way, but I will be more careful about teasing from here on out." James steadied a box on the wagon.

"Elizabeth isn't usually that sensitive; she just has to get to know you."

"You're a lucky man, Scott. You have a beautiful, talented wife and you should be a happy man."

"I am. I can tell you, I know how fortunate I am."

CHAPTER 20

The month of April was fast approaching and Elizabeth and Scott were all settled in their new home. Elizabeth was busy with the nursery, but not knowing what the baby would be, she painted the walls a soft yellow. Stepping back, she looked at her work.

"Well, that does look quite nice if I do say so myself."

At the onset of Elizabeth's pregnancy, Scott experienced morning sickness and now, near her delivery date, he was having stomach cramps. Elizabeth did not know whether she thought it was sweet or an inconvenience.

"You know when a man gets sick, it's a major production." She was talking about the plans for the delivery with her mother. "I don't know what kind of discomfort he will feel when the baby is actually being born."

The doctor did not expect any complications with the delivery. He had told Scott on many occasions that his wife was in very good health, and he was not to worry about Elizabeth.

"I don't know that Scott will be much help with the baby; he's such a baby himself when it comes to some things."

"Elizabeth, he will rise to the occasion, I promise."

"There's really not too much left to do. Everything seems

to be ready to welcome this little one and, believe me, I am surely ready."

"Do you have a name for boy or girl, Elizabeth?"

"Yes, mam, I do."

"Well, am I privileged enough to hear them?"

"Not now, I haven't even discussed it with Scott. You will just have to wait, mama."

"I'll just try and guess what you chose. You know that my middle name is Rose." Her mother laughed.

"I was thinking Rosy Belle, mama. What do you think about Rosy Belle? That would be your name and Scott's mother's name also. I could kill two birds with one stone."

"On second thought, maybe you had best look elsewhere for a name."

Scott had forbidden Elizabeth to do any more painting because of the fumes from the paint. He thought that it could be harmful for the baby. As a result of his decision, the crib was left unfinished. Scott was to do it himself, but as yet, had not found the extra time.

"Your father would love to come over and finish the job on the crib."

"I don't want to ask him to do that, mama."

"I'm sure that he would be thrilled to do it. It would make him feel more a part of this event. You know, sometimes men feel a little left out when it comes to women having babies."

"Well, Scott Gilmore is not among that number. He is a little too much involved sometimes."

"He just wants to make sure that you are all right. Personally, I am very happy that he's that way."

Elizabeth and her mother had a nice, long visit until the afternoon when Mrs. Buie left. Scott came home a little earlier than usual that day.

"Good heavens, Scott, I haven't even started dinner. Why are you home so soon?"

"I just wanted to check on the little mother to see if you were feeling okay."

"Dear, I'm healthy as a horse."

"That's good to know, but I just wanted to make sure."

"Mother said that she would get dad to come over and finish up any painting that still needs to be done."

Scott looked disappointed. "I'm planning on doing that. I just haven't had time lately."

"I know how busy you are and that's one reason that it makes perfect sense to let dad do it. Another reason is that it would let him feel that he is a bigger part of the birth of his first grandchild."

"Oh, I hadn't thought of that. You may be right about that. We can let him do that, if that's what he wants to do."

The days seemed to fly by for Scott and drag for Elizabeth, but be that as it may, mid-April had arrived and no baby had come. On the eve of Easter, Elizabeth had decided that it was time for her to begin making Jesus cookies herself, since she was soon to be a mother and would tell the Easter story to her own child. Taking her mother's recipe in hand, she assembled all the ingredients that she would need. Remembering that the oven needed to be preheated before the cookies were put in, she lit the stove. She hummed a little tune as she whipped the egg whites. When they were the right consistency, she greased the cookie pan and dropped mounds of the snowy white confection onto the sheet. Placing the cookies into the oven and closing the oven door, she turned off the stove and put the tape across the front, as a reminder to herself not to open it until Easter morning. Elizabeth was feeling quite pleased with her first attempt at making Jesus cookies.

Scott was asleep, but she found it impossible to get to sleep.

She went into the parlor and sat down with a book she had chosen from her collection. Suddenly, she had a sharp pain that made her sit up very straight.

"What was that? Do you suppose someone is trying to tell you something?" Elizabeth was talking to herself. She waited several minutes. "False alarm, I guess." Upon opening her book, she had another twinge. She put the book aside and thought to herself, "I wish I knew more about how this is supposed to work. Maybe I should wake Scott. What about the Jesus cookies? Oh, they are fine, the oven is off." Her mind was rolling a mile a minute as she tried to remember all the things she needed to do. At long last, she decided to wake Scott. Walking quietly into the bedroom and sitting on the edge of the bed next to Scott, she touched him softly on the shoulder. His reaction nearly knocked Elizabeth to the floor. Rubbing his sleepy eyes, he looked at Elizabeth.

"Sweetheart, are you in pain? Is it time to get the doctor?" He fairly jumped to the other side of the bed so he would not knock Elizabeth over, and began to put on his clothes.

"Oh, I knew I wouldn't be ready when the time came. I need to think what I was supposed to do first." Scott was going in circles.

"Scott, we have plenty of time. I'm not even sure that the pains are the baby. I may have gas or something else that's causing my discomfort."

"It has to be the baby. I'll go for the doctor immediately."

"No, you will not! You will calm down and come into the parlor and wait with me until we are sure."

Scott finished dressing and followed Elizabeth into the parlor.

"While we are waiting, I need to discuss names for the baby with you. What do you think...?" Her words trailed off as she looked down to see that her water had broken.

"Scott, it's time to get the doctor. My water just broke."

Scott was out the front door and down the steps before Elizabeth could say another word.

"Well, I wish he had waited until I told him to go and tell mama to come over."

In no time at all Scott was back, pushing Dr. Jobe up the steps as he went. "Hurry up, Doc."

"Scott, Elizabeth has got a while to go before that baby comes. It's bad enough having to run to keep up with you. I'm glad you came in the buggy or I wouldn't have been physically able to deliver your child."

"Come on, doc!"

Dr. Jobe could only shake his head, hoping once they got inside, Scott would turn his motor off. Elizabeth was on the couch smiling up at them as they entered.

"Hello, Dr. Jobe. Sorry to awaken you at this hour, but this little one is getting over anxious."

"Don't give it a second thought. It's really Scott who needs a doctor."

Elizabeth nodded her head and then addressed Scott.

"Scott, would you please go and get mama and bring her over here?"

"What?"

"I want mama here for this birthing."

"I can't leave you in all this pain and miss the birth of my first child."

Dr. Jobe smiled. "I promise you that you won't miss a thing. These little ones take hours sometimes. Go get your mother-in-law. If you don't you will have two women upset with you and, trust me, you don't want that to happen."

Reluctantly, Scott ran from the house to the buggy and turned in the direction of the Buie's home. Dr. Jobe went on to examine Elizabeth and her progress. Elizabeth had moved into the bedroom and changed into a fresh gown.

"We are going to be several hours yet unless this young gentleman or lady wakes up."

Elizabeth heard the screen bang shut and Scott rushed into the room. "Is the baby here? Did I miss anything?"

"Dr. Jobe says we will be an hour or more before this baby decides it wants to meet us."

Mrs. Buie walked into the room with her robe buttoned in the wrong sequence and her hair uncombed.

"My stars, mama, you look as though you were in a hurry."

"Scott told me that the baby was being born, and I didn't even have time to comb my hair. Then when we came inside, Scott literally slammed the door in my face. I'm still a bit rattled by the near miss."

"Scott, you need to get control of yourself," Elizabeth was trying hard to control her laughter at the two before her. "This is quite a picture. I wish the two of you could see yourselves. Mama, you wouldn't be caught dead looking as you do right now, and Scott, you act like an escapee from an asylum." Both Elizabeth and Dr. Jobe were laughing, which relieved the tension for Scott somewhat.

"I will fix a pot of coffee," mama said and headed for the kitchen.

At about three-thirty in the morning and two pots of coffee, Dr. Jobe had Mrs. Buie usher Scott out of the bedroom and at three-forty a tiny cry was heard by Scott and grandmother through the door. Dr. Jobe asked Mrs. Buie to come in and help him with the cleanup duties, but Scott must wait outside until the baby was all cleaned up and happy.

Elizabeth called for Scott through the door. He entered the room almost reverently to see the tiny, red, little one all wrapped up and lying in Elizabeth's arms. The joy was overwhelming and unashamed tears rolled down his face. He approached the bed and with all looking on, Elizabeth announced, "I want to present to you, Miss Charlotte Royal Gilmore," and she smiled.

CHAPTER 21

*C*harlotte grew quickly. She did not have red hair nor look anything like her name sake, but each time Elizabeth looked at her angelic face, she remembered her childhood friend. She was a happy baby and to Scott's great delight, his little daughter smiled each time she saw his face. Scott picked up his daughter from the crib.

"Do you know who is going to be one year old this week?"

Charlotte had learned to make the motor boat noise, thanks to her father, and she made it at the mention of her very first birthday.

"Well, if that's the way you feel about it, Miss blue eyes, you may not get that pony I was thinking about getting you."

Elizabeth overheard and walked into the nursery. "I can tell you, she won't be getting a pony."

"I was just teasing her, Elizabeth. I'm thinking more along the lines of a puppy." "You are impossible."

"What kind of a party are you thinking about having for our Charlotte? How about clowns and a juggler or two?"

"Scott!"

"No, it would really be great. We could write an article for the paper about Charlotte's first birthday."

"Who are we inviting? The president?"

"I'm just picking at you, Elizabeth, but we could mention her birthday in the paper, like in the community news."

"I am so embarrassed." Elizabeth walked back into the kitchen shaking her head. "You know, of course, that Charlotte won't even remember her one year birthday party." Elizabeth could not help but tell Scott.

"How do you know?" Scott called.

"Tell me, Scott, do you remember yours?"

"No, I don't, but Charlotte is so much smarter than I am."

The party turned out to be slightly less than daddy Scott had anticipated, but Charlotte was lovely in her new blue frock to match her blue eyes and her white hair bow which was almost as big as her head. Both grandma's and grandpa's were present, along with James from the paper. There was cake and ice cream and Jesus cookies, of course. James had become a frequent visitor at the Gilmore house and quite a friend to Scott. Scott didn't want to think of how he would survive at the paper without James to help. He had, at long last, decided that he would do a little more writing along the sports line. This demanded a bit more research on the teams with which he had been familiar years earlier as well as the current teams in baseball. Although he enjoyed it quite a bit, he felt that it took up too much of his time, which made his regular chores suffer.

"Look, James, it's important to me and to the paper that we expand a little more. Elizabeth has told me that she wants to get back into her story writing and that can be done in her spare time at home. I think it's important for you to take the time you need to get back in touch with the thing you love to do. I won't be footing the bill for any long train trips you have to take to accomplish this though."

James smiled at Scott and knew that he was sincere about his getting back in touch with what he did best and loved most.

"I guess I could give it a try. I would like to see what ole Matthew is up to and how his little wife is doing. She was pretty sickly at one point in time. He's a good kid and was devastated when he messed up his elbow. I think it would be worth writing something like a 'where are they now' article."

"I think that would be great."

"I know lots of those guys whose careers were cut short because of injury. Maybe there are folks who are curious about what happened to them."

"Bet you are right. Do you know many more besides this Matthew guy?"

"Quite a few, but he is the one I followed more closely. This kid was made for greatness. Rhythm on second was a beauty to watch and had the highest batting average in the league. I think he grew up around here or maybe it was his wife. No, I'm wrong because he grew up in Mississippi. He would be a good start though. For a while Matthew was a sports analyst for some paper close by. I don't know what he is doing now, but I could feel him out and see how he feels about a job with us."

"Don't think I could afford another writer just now, but it's a good idea."

"I'm really reaching. I don't even know where the guy is now. So many years have gone by."

Elizabeth came into the parlor with the coffee server on a little tray with pieces of her pecan pie. She had become quite good at baking pecan pie and even better at making Jesus cookies.

"I thought you two might like a snack and a coffee pick me up. I am writing a short little story for the paper to see if I still have it. It ought to be ready in time to go into this week's paper."

Scott smiled. "Can't wait to read it."

Elizabeth left the men to their conversation and went to the nursery. Charlotte was in the midst of an afternoon nap and Elizabeth decided that it would be a good time to write. She was excited about getting back into her old job. She sat down at her desk with paper and pencil and began.

"Have you ever had a friend, such a friend that you could confidently tell her all your inner most secrets and not have a fear that she would ever tell? I had that friend. We played together, ate together, dreamed together and there was no seam between us. Like sisters, we went on adventures together, with each one wanting the other to have just the same amount of fun. We laughed together, a lot! We didn't seem to need anyone else. As a matter of fact, I didn't want to share her nor did she want to share me.

Through the war, we were agreeable, even though some friends were killing each other just because they lived in different places or had some idea of a great cause that they shared or didn't share. People on one side would wonder what the cause was all about. They wondered about what their cause was as well. My friend and I didn't care about causes, we only knew that we loved one another, and that was the important thing. Until that day, that day that came so unexpectedly. I offended my friend deeply and when she left, I didn't ever hear from her again. I discovered that there was a hole in our otherwise solid armor. It was a hole that I could never repair because it was a part of my soul, and hers went that deeply also. It seemed that neither of us could remove ourselves from what we believed on such a personal level, and so, we are still parted.

In my prayers, I always pray that I will have the chance to see her once more and tell her that I am sorry for offending her, but I could never tell her that I agree with her very personal soul belief. I found that day that we were different, and I never believed that we were. Can two people be that much alike, and yet that much different? Can you be their friend and not share your good news with them? I look back at that moment now and have a different idea about what I did. At the time, I did it out of ignorance, but now I would do it again out of love. God bless you, my friend."

Elizabeth walked into the parlor and James was gone. She handed her article to Scott. "This one is not like the usual ones, so maybe you had better proof it."

"Sweetheart, you wrote from deep within your soul. I think it's a lesson that so many need to hear. When you've got good news, you need to share it."

"Scott, I've written this story before, but now I know the reason that I don't feel the need to apologize for telling the story of the Jesus cookies. I feel a burden has been removed from my heart."

CHAPTER 22

When James walked into the office that next week, Scott let him read Elizabeth's article.

"This is the friend that Elizabeth had during her childhood. She has wanted me, for years, to try and find her. She is who our baby is named for."

"Man, what a friendship that must have been for her to be pursuing it for so long."

"Why was her friend so offended?"

"Elizabeth shared the story of the Jesus cookies with her."

"So why was she so offended? That doesn't sound right."

"She told Elizabeth that she was Jewish, and she did not want her religion to be blamed for killing Christ."

"I see, and Elizabeth didn't know that her friend was Jewish."

"Her family moved away shortly after that and Elizabeth didn't know where they went."

"That's a sad story, but she did a great job with the article."

"It's not her best, but I know that this one came from deep down, and it's going in the paper this week."

"Listen, I think I am going to visit with the guy we were talking about, you know, Matthew. I called a friend of mine and found out that he lives not fifty miles from here. That's not too far, and it wouldn't take me long to get a quick interview. I'd like to see how his wife is doing also."

"That would be great, and we'll see if we can get it in next week's paper."

"We will see how people respond, and maybe get some mileage out of it."

James seemed to be pleased and left to make plans for his trip to Thomastown. During James' two day absence from the paper, things got hectic for Scott. Elizabeth left Charlotte with her mother for one day and worked with Scott for a few hours. Grandma enjoyed Charlotte's short visit and asked Elizabeth to do it again soon. Elizabeth didn't like being away from Charlotte and decided then and there that she could not ever go back to work full time.

When James returned the next day, Scott told him that he had really been missed and that he might not be able to spare him for trips very often.

"I'm very interested to know what you found out."

James relayed his information.

"Matthew was playing ball in the majors, like I told you, when he messed up his elbow. He went to all kinds of doctors, and they basically told him that he would never have the same range of motion that he had in that arm and that he wouldn't have the same amount of strength. As you know, you have to have good motion in your arm to play ball. There were plenty of guys waiting in the wings to fill that spot, so they dropped him. He decided to go back to school and get his degree. While he was there, he met and married his wife. I went to visit her there also. He was about to bring her home because the doctors in the hospital had done all they could do for her. I felt like they were just sending her home to die. Anyway, he has some little job that doesn't pay much at all, but gives him the time off he needs to care for his wife. They have a little girl, and Matthew's mother helps with her when Matthew can't be at home. Can you imagine being in that kind of situation?"

Scott's head was down, thinking about Matthew's life in general.

"How is the wife's outlook on her condition? Didn't it depress you to go in to talk with her?"

"No, she had the most positive outlook on her life, such as it was. She cheered me up with her positive attitude. She looked tired, but she had a big smile on her face. She has beautiful red hair, and it was combed neatly. You think of people who are bed-ridden as letting themselves go and just not caring about appearance. Evidently, that was not her cup of tea."

Scott wanted to help Matthew if he possibly could but could not decide how he would do it. "You know, I would like to help Matthew out. He sounds like such a deserving person. I couldn't pay him a big salary at the paper, but I do think I could allow him time to help with his wife and maybe an extra day or two to make money on the side."

James smiled, "I don't know how much money he makes, but it couldn't be very much. There may be a way I can find out if you want me to."

Scott asked James if there might be some way he could talk with Matthew. James said he would try. By the next week, James was well under way with his contacts with Matthew and had found a way for Matthew to come meet with Scott.

"He will be in town to meet you Tuesday if that's okay with you, Scott."

"That's fine. I'm flexible, but he will have to meet me here at the office."

James was excited. "I'll see he gets here. He's excited to meet you."

"I'll be planning on spending some time getting to know

Matthew on Tuesday." James thought Tuesday would never come, but it did. James walked into the office with a tall, slender young man, who appeared to be about Scott's own age. "Scott, this is Matthew. Matthew, this is Scott, my boss."

"I don't think we have determined who the boss is at this point, Matthew, but I have heard all kinds of good things about you. I am very happy to meet you. What has James said to you about the purpose of our meeting?"

"He told me that just maybe you had a job offer for me."

"I really don't know what you make or if you would be interested in a job with my paper, but I hear that you are very good at what you do and I do need help."

"My wife used to live here a very long time ago, and I believe that she would be most happy to return here to live and raise our little girl."

"Let's see what we can work out. Are you interested, Matthew?"

"I do think I would like to see if we could work it out."

James quietly slipped out and kept his fingers crossed that this would be for the benefit of both of his friends. When he left, Scott was talking about the apartment that he and Elizabeth had occupied being available, because he had purchased it when the owner moved. Matthew said that he would have to talk with his wife about the move, but he would let him know of his decision very soon. The two shook hands and Matthew left to go back to Thomastown.

It had been a long, hard day for Scott, but he came in, kissed Elizabeth and began to look for Charlotte. "Where's my girl?" he called. He heard a little squeal coming from the nursery. "I hear you, little girl," he called out. Another squeal. "I'm coming to get you!"

Elizabeth laughed as Scott appeared in the doorway with Charlotte patting his face.

"You two are so silly."

"Yeah, but you love us."

"Indeed, I do."

"Sweetheart, I met with that young man with the sick wife today. I hope I can get him something to do here at the paper."

"Where did you say he lived?"

"In Thomastown. It's only about fifty miles from here. He said that his wife used to live here a long time ago."

"What was her last name?"

"Oh, I don't know. I didn't even think to ask him. He is a real nice guy though. I just hope I can help him out. He has had such a sad life."

"Wish you would ask their last name when you see him. Mama may know who they are." As Elizabeth was taking off her apron, there was a knock at the door. "Scott, can you get that, please?"

He walked to the door with Charlotte in his arms. A young boy stood at the screen out of breath, as if he had been running.

"You okay, son?"

"Yes, sir," he said, "Dr. Jobe sent me to tell you that Mr. Buie is in the hospital and not doing well. Doc Jobe thinks he may have had a heart attack."

"What hospital?"

"County General. It's near Gunter, about ten miles away."

"I know the place. Thank you, son."

Elizabeth had walked into the parlor and asked Scott who the company had been.

"Elizabeth, I want you to be calm. Your father seems to have had a mild heart attack. He is in the hospital being taken care of by Dr. Jobe. Get your shawl and some things for the baby. I will drive us there. It's only ten miles from here, so we will get there very quickly."

Scott was surprised by his wife's reaction to the news. It

may have been Scott's calm demeanor that soothed her. He did not know, but was relieved that she had not overreacted. Soon Elizabeth had gathered all she needed for the short trip and they were on the way. Elizabeth got out of the carriage first, leaving Scott to gather the baby's needs. She hurried inside to find her mother in a wooden straight chair at the foot of her father's bed.

"How is he, mama? Have they given him anything?"

"I really don't know what they have given him, but he seems to be resting comfortably now. He had some awful pain, Elizabeth."

Elizabeth put her arm around her mother's shoulder and patted her lovingly.

"Where is Charlotte, Elizabeth?"

"Oh, she and Scott will be here in a minute. I left him to get all Charlotte's things and bring them in with her."

Scott appeared at the door with a smiling Charlotte. She reached for her grandmother when she saw her. Mrs. Buie rose from the chair to take her. Giving her a peck on her rosy cheek, she sat back down in the chair.

"Your grandpa would be so glad you came to see him."

Charlotte smiled as she touched her grandmother's face and patted her cheek.

Mr. Buie made a slight grunting sound as he turned more to his side.

Charlotte joined in by making the motor boat sound. Mr. Buie's eyes open and seeing Charlotte, he smiled.

"Oh, me, I have died and gone to heaven because I see an angel over there."

Charlotte reached for her grandfather and he reached back.

"Now, daddy, you can't hold her. You've just had some kind of heart spasm."

"I'm fine. I just got indigestion from your mama's cooking."

"Neil, you did no such thing!"

He laughed and continued to make noises at Charlotte who would always respond with the motor boat sound.

"You two are disrupting the whole hospital. We need to tone it down." Elizabeth was afraid that her father would get fatigued and his heart would react again. She could not bring herself to say the words, 'heart attack'."

Elizabeth felt secure in knowing that her father was going to be fine, and it would be just a little while until he would be going home. She gathered up Charlotte's things and kissed her father on the cheek.

"You behave yourself and maybe they will let you leave. We have to get Miss Priss home and into bed. She has done enough traveling today." She kissed her mother on the cheek and left.

They had been driving for only about five minutes when Charlotte was fast asleep.

"Scott, I want to know about this family of Matthew's and what I can do to help them. I can't imagine what I would do if I couldn't care for Charlotte. Where did you say he lived?"

"He's from Thomastown."

"Where in the world is Thomastown?"

"It's in Mississippi."

"Well, he's a long way from Mississippi up here. Wonder what he's doing way up here?"

"Elizabeth, he came here to go to the university, but got into the major league baseball scene. Why are you so interested?"

"I don't know, but I want you to find out what her folks last name is please."

"I promise I will as soon as I talk with him again."

From that point, the ride home was mostly silent. When they got home, Elizabeth put Charlotte to bed and went into the parlor.

"I don't know why I'm so interested in these people unless it makes me so thankful for how God has blessed me and my family." She put her head back against the big chair in the parlor and went sound asleep.

CHAPTER 23

Elizabeth woke up the next morning fully intending to begin a project she had been thinking about almost as soon as she found out that she was expecting a baby. With Charlotte down for a nap, she sat down in the parlor and began to write on the material for her book. She had decided to write a series of little poems and limericks for children. She had already committed some to memory and she began with what she thought to be her best limerick.

"There was an old man from Natchez,
Who sat on a big box of matches.
The matches caught fire,
And burned his attire;
And now he goes round in patches."

She sat back and read what she had written with a smile. "Not too bad," she thought to herself. "But it's so short. How could I ever come up with enough of these to make up a book, even a short one?" It was then that she had what she thought was a wonderful idea. If she could get enough people interested in having their own little poems or rhymes printed, she just might be able to get this children's book to happen. She needed a plan and it didn't take Elizabeth long to formulate one. She took her pencil and wrote across the top of a fresh sheet of paper, "CONTEST." She had in mind the idea of the paper holding a contest for best poems or short verses with a prize being presented to the winner. The paper could print the book. The extra plus would be that the work would be printed as first place winner in a children's book along with the other offerings from the readers.

Elizabeth was proud of her idea and quite eager to show it to Scott. Another up-side would be that the paper could print the books and make money on the sale of them. She knew that the people who had their works published were sure to purchase at least one book. That afternoon, as soon as Scott opened the front door, Elizabeth escorted him by the arm and began to try and explain her idea. "Wait a minute, sweetheart, let me sit down and catch my breath." Wearily, he made his way to the big overstuffed chair. "I'm worn out, Elizabeth. You sure this can't wait till after dinner?"

"I suppose it could, but if I waited to tell you, I probably would burst."

"Well, we can't have that happen. What's so all fired important? You're not pregnant again, are you?"

"No, it's nothing like that. This is along the line of how the paper can get more revenue."

"I just know this is going to be good."

Elizabeth eyed her husband harshly. "You are going to be so sorry you didn't come up with this idea. I was thinking that we could have a contest, sponsored by the paper, in which we award a prize for one of our reader's best article submitted."

"You want me to let the public write articles for the paper?"

"No, silly, it's a contest in which they submit poems or limericks to be judged by us. We would then use them to put into a little children's book. The best part is that we could print the books and sell them to all the people who wrote something. You know they would want a book with their own work printed inside."

"How do you know who would buy one? If we misjudged on the number, we would actually lose money on the printing."

"I have thought of that, Mr. Editor, and I say we take orders before we go to print on our little books."

"Sounds as if you have been doing a lot of thinking about this idea of yours. Who do you suppose we could put in charge of your little project?"

"Maybe that Matthew guy, if he decides to come and, if not, I might be able to do most of the footwork from home."

"Sweetheart, I like your idea, but I sort of need to work through some of the areas that I see as being potential problems. Good job, though, it's one of the best ideas I've heard in a while."

"Are you serious, Scott? Do you really think I have a good idea here? That makes my day."

"Well, make mine and feed me! I'm just two inches from starving to death."

At the dinner table, Elizabeth did not interrupt Scott with any further explanations about her idea or even why she thought that it would work. The main thing for Elizabeth was that her husband liked her idea and acknowledgment pleased her immensely.

Scott left the table with a compliment on the dinner, which was his usual custom, and went straight to the nursery and his little one.

"There you are, Miss Priss."

Charlotte threw her toy out of the crib and showed that infectious grin, the same one that Elizabeth loved so much about Scott.

"You been here all day? Well, daddy will fix that right now."

Scott swung Charlotte over the railing of the crib, which

led to delighted giggles from her. Sitting in the rocker in the corner, Scott placed her on his knee. Holding both of her arms, he began to bounce her and sing.

"Ride a horsey, ride a horsey, down to town. Better be careful or you might fall down." With that last line, he collapsed his knee and Charlotte squealed in delight as she dropped.

Elizabeth watched lovingly from the door of the nursery and thought, "How blessed I am to have such a perfect family." As she was counting her blessings, she also thought of Matthew's life and all the trials he had encountered. It was hard for her to even imagine being in that situation. An invalid wife and a small child and not much of a job for their support. Elizabeth thought that his wife must be an unusually strong person. She couldn't figure which one would need more strength to endure that condition.

Scott rocked Charlotte until she fell sleep in his arms. He laid her in her crib to sleep for the night and went into the parlor. He walked to the sofa and sat down next to Elizabeth, where she was still in thought about Matthew's family.

"Tell me again what you know about Matthew's family. I just can't seem to get them off my mind."

"I know it's difficult to think about without becoming depressed, but Matthew is one of the most upbeat young men I have ever met. I have not heard from him about the job, but I can tell you what James has told me. According to James, the wife has a wonderful disposition as well."

"What else has James said?"

"I have told you, Elizabeth. Matthew is from Thomastown, came here to our state to go to university, and there met and married his wife. He got into the major leagues and while there, messed up his elbow. James says he could have been a great professional baseball player."

"What else, Scott? How did his wife get sick? What is her disease?"

"I don't know that, Elizabeth, but has something to do with her blood, I think."

"Maybe we will know more when you hear from him about the job."

"Oh, there's something else that I forgot. I thought it was very interesting that they have a little girl, and guess what? Her name is Elizabeth!"

CHAPTER 24

Elizabeth was wrapped up in her idea for a newspaper contest. She was working on how to word the announcement for the paper. Scott had given her his approval to begin the project and she went into the planning whole heartedly. The contest announcement came out in the paper the following week, and Elizabeth could hardly wait to see the response.

"Elizabeth, I think you have created a monster," Scott said upon entering the house for lunch.

"What do you mean, Scott?"

"It's only been three days since the contest began, and we are swamped with people bringing in their little poems and stories."

Elizabeth clapped her hands and smiled. "I can't wait to begin reading them." "Well, if traffic gets any heavier with people coming into the office while we are trying to work, you may have to get your mother to keep Charlotte and help us out."

On the following day, Elizabeth was back at her old desk collecting poems and stories. "Scott, I think we will have to put a deadline on the submissions."

"Good idea. How about yesterday?"

"Print a little sign for the front window saying that tomorrow will be the last day for submitting their work."

"By the way, I think Matthew is coming to work for the paper. I asked him what his wife's last name was."

"Well, what did he say?"

"It was a strange name, Goldstein, I believe."

"I'll ask mama if she knew them, but I have never known anybody by that name here." Picking up all the contributions from the readers, Elizabeth headed for home and a very long night of reading.

Mrs. Buie was playing with Charlotte on the floor. She laughed as Elizabeth entered.

"Don't laugh, this pile of papers is going to give us a lift with our income."

"I wasn't laughing at you, Elizabeth. I was laughing at the mental picture of me getting up from this floor."

For added effect, Charlotte made the motor boat sound.

"Well, that was right on cue. Your mama will think we practiced that!"

"Now that's funny."

Elizabeth went to her desk and put all the papers down. Stacking them in as orderly a fashion as possible, she turned to her mother.

"Do you remember anyone from here by the name of Goldstein?"

Her mother shook her head, "No, I don't believe I do. How long ago was that, Elizabeth?"

"I don't know, mama, but I think we would have remembered that name if we had known them."

"Why do you ask, dear?"

"It's just that Matthew and his family will be moving here, just down the street into the Gasson's old place, and I haven't met Matthew's wife. I had hoped to establish some sort of point for conversation when we do meet."

"That's a good idea. I have lived here for forty years and used to pride myself in thinking I knew every family in this town. It's just odd that I don't remember them."

"Mother, it's a small town, but I really don't believe you know every family that lives here."

Mrs. Buie rolled over onto her knees and, holding to the chair, rose from the floor to her full height.

"Mother, how un-lady like!"

"I told you that I was getting old, Elizabeth."

Elizabeth was smiling at her mother, but inwardly felt badly because of possibly offending her mother. "My mouth is my own worst enemy, but it's because my brain doesn't think before my mouth speaks." Elizabeth found herself once again thinking back to the day she offended and lost her best friend.

Elizabeth's mother went home, and Elizabeth took time to cuddle for a while with Charlotte and then rocked her to sleep. She knew that Scott would have a late night at the paper, so she fixed her a cup of tea and sat down at her desk to tackle the mountain of papers before her. After about an hour of reading, she moved to the more comfortable overstuffed chair in the parlor. Mohammed was not moving much of the mountain, and Elizabeth went to the kitchen for a refill on her tea cup.

Scott came in tired from his long day at the paper.

"You look exhausted, Scott."

"I am a little bit tired. I think I'll have a sandwich and go to bed."

Elizabeth didn't question his decision, even though she wanted to talk with him about the poems she had read.

The next morning Charlotte was up at her usual time of six, ready for breakfast.

"Oh, Miss Charlotte," she said smiling, "I will be so very glad when you decide to sleep till eight or nine in the morning."

Scott came into the kitchen and sat down at the table. "I feel so refreshed this morning. Thanks for letting me go straight to bed last night. I know you had a dozen questions about the contest."

"No, not really about the contest, but I do have a couple about Matthew and his family. I was wondering how his wife is doing."

"I understand that she is back in the hospital. They are trying a new procedure and hope that it will give her some comfort. This is the reason I have not heard from Matthew in so long."

"Oh, I'm so sorry. Do they think that the procedure will help with a cure?"

"I don't know, sweetheart. I guess they are ready to try anything at this point. Oh, yes, about his wife's name, James told me that the name Goldstein is a Jewish name and they changed it. The name here was Gasson."

Elizabeth dropped the spoon that she had been using to cook the eggs.

"Scott, that's Charlotte! It's Charlotte!" Elizabeth burst into tears.

Scott rushed to her side just as she was about to faint. Leaning on Scott's strong shoulder, Elizabeth continued to weep. Whether it was for joy or sorrow, she could not tell.

"Elizabeth, you can't be sure."

"Just as sure as I am that we are standing here. It couldn't be anyone else. I'll bet you would find, if you asked, that she has bright red hair."

"Now that you mention it, I remember James saying her hair was beautiful and it is red."

"Scott, I have to see her as soon as possible."

"I will find out where she is and how you can go to see her. Just let me talk with Matthew."

The day had come to an end, but Elizabeth knew that she would be unable to sleep. Her mind was filled with questions about her friend and why she had not heard from her. She wondered how she would be received when she went to see Charlotte. Elizabeth tossed and wondered until almost dawn. When she awoke, it was as though yesterday had never even ended. She still had the same things to ask Charlotte, the same plea for forgiveness and the utmost desire for acceptance of her heartfelt plea. "Oh, dear Lord in heaven, grant me this one plea for forgiveness and acceptance of my friendship by Charlotte." Walking through the house, her mind was still racing. "How could I have missed this? Matthew is a boy from Mississippi, wife's family lived here earlier, he met her at the university, Jewish name, and the red hair!" True, she had not known about the red hair until last night, but she should have known it was Charlotte. "Mama will keep Charlotte for me, and I can go by train if it's too far to drive." At long last, Elizabeth felt her prayer to see her childhood friend once again had been answered.

CHAPTER 25

Scott came directly home after he found out from James that Charlotte was in a very upscale hospital in Raleigh. Charlotte's parents must have had a hand in that, but if that's where Charlotte needed to be, they would want to put her there.

Elizabeth made arrangements for her mother and father to keep Charlotte for a couple of days while Elizabeth went to see her friend. Scott wanted to go with Elizabeth, but could find no way, short of closing down the paper, to make that happen. Elizabeth packed her overnight bag and sent James to the depot to purchase her ticket to Raleigh.

"I have told Matthew that you want to meet his wife and will be arriving at the hospital tomorrow some time. I said nothing else about your trip. I felt that you would want to explain that to him."

"Thank you, James."

The next morning, Elizabeth was taken to the station early by Scott.

"Elizabeth, I want you to be strong. You have no idea how you will be received by Charlotte. It's been a long time since you two have talked."

"I know, Scott, I have been preparing myself for the possibility of rejection, but I have prayed that it won't happen."

"Okay, let's go to the station."

It seemed that the buggy was extra slow going down the street. Elizabeth wondered if they may be late for the train, and she could not endure the possibility of having to wait another day to see Charlotte.

They actually arrived ten minutes early.

"I should have known that you would get me here on time. You are always thinking for me. I love you so much, Scott."

"All I ask is that you not expect too much. Prepare yourself for the worse, and if it's something good, you will be okay."

The train's shrill whistle could be heard around the bend. Belching smoke, it screeched to a half at the station. It put Elizabeth in remembrance of the day Charlotte went off to college and out of her life. It left a feeling of regret inside Elizabeth.

"Oh, no you don't," she thought. "Nothing negative is to enter your thoughts." "Board!" The conductor was calling for the passengers.

Elizabeth made her way toward the train. Giving the conductor her bag, she stepped onto the little stool and then onto the train. With Scott still steadying her by holding her arm, she looked at him lovingly. "Good-bye, my love. I will see you in a couple of days."

The train pulled out of the station for the trip to Raleigh. Elizabeth had taken a seat beside the window and smiled at Scott on the platform until he was out of sight. She had not realized how tired she was and laid her head against the seat watching the trees go by until she had fallen asleep.

"Raleigh station," the conductor announced their next stop.

Elizabeth got her bag and held it close against her chest. She did not know whether it was to keep her from forgetting it or to keep her from shaking. The train rolled to a stop and the conductor reached for Elizabeth's hand to help her off the train. She found a buggy close by and hired it to take her to the hospital. It seemed like a long ride, but probably lasted no more than five or six minutes. Elizabeth hesitated for only a moment, and then stepped down, and taking her bag walked through the front door of the Lady of Love Catholic Hospital. The hospital was small and smelled of antiseptic. Elizabeth was looking for room five.

"Oh, here we are!" Taking a peek around the open door, she saw a frail little figure surrounded by a halo of red hair. "Oh, my poor, dear friend," she thought. Realizing that someone had entered her room, Charlotte opened her eyes. Elizabeth's heart almost leaped from her chest. Gathering her courage, Elizabeth took a few more steps inside the room.

"Well, aren't you the lazy one? It's a beautiful day outside. We could have a china berry war."

"Elizabeth? Can that be you? Oh, Elizabeth."

"Charlotte, it's been so long. I didn't know what happened to you. I never got to tell you good-bye or how sorry that I was to have offended you. I knew you married a boy from Mississippi, but I never heard from you. I found out that you have a little girl, and I assumed you named her Elizabeth after your old friend. Do you want to know something else? I have a little girl also, and her name is Charlotte."

"Elizabeth, just after I met and married Matthew, I got sick and we went all over the place trying to find out what was wrong with me. Then I had Elizabeth and she took up my time."

"I know I offended you with the story of the Jesus cookies, but I did not know you were Jewish."

"Elizabeth, if you will slow down a little, I have something to tell you. I know you remember how much I enjoyed eating those Jesus cookies, and I asked you to tell me the meaning behind them."

"Yes, and I offended you, but I couldn't seem to find a way to fix it."

"Elizabeth, what you said that day about the Jesus cookies changed my life. I met a man called Jesus!"

With tears welling up in her eyes and spilling down her cheeks, she moved to Charlotte's bed and took her hand. Charlotte smiled up at her old friend and said, "I just have to thank you for those Jesus cookies and what that empty tomb has meant to me."

Squeezing Charlotte's frail hand slightly, Elizabeth smiled at her friend through her tears, and softly whispered, "Tell it, Charlotte."

JESUS COOKIES

2 egg white
2/3 cup sugar
Pinch of salt
1/8 tsp. cream of tartar
1 tsp. vanilla
1 cup chopped pecans

Pre-heat oven to 350 degrees.
Beat egg whites until peaks begin to form.
Gradually add sugar as you beat whites.
Add salt and cream of tartar and vanilla.
Stir in broken pecans.
Drop cookies by teaspoon onto foil lined pan.
Place in oven and turn off heat.
Place tape across oven door and do not open until Easter morning (the next morning).
Share cookies and the story with children and friends.
HE IS NOT HERE!! HE IS RISEN!!!

ABOUT THE AUTHOR

Sarah (Kelly) Albritton is the mother of five and grandmother of eleven. She has a bachelor's degree from Belhaven College and a master's degree in English. Sarah loves family history and has a deep love of her Scottish Presbyterian roots. She is retired and lives in Clinton, Mississippi, where she has lived for the last forty-two years.